"I need to talk now," sh

He turned, clearly stunned that she had not obeyed his command to just follow him home. But she was done waiting and keeping this secret to herself. There was no right time to say it, so she just said it.

"I'm pregnant."

Nick slowly turned all the way around to face her, his eyes never wavering. Silvia practically held her breath.

"Nick?" she finally said.

"Meet me at my house."

And with that he turned and got into his truck and drove off. Looked like she would be following his command after all, but then the first order of business would be teaching Nick Campbell that she didn't take orders from anyone.

* * *

An Unexpected Scandal by Jules Bennett is a part of the Lockwood Lightning series.

Dear Reader,

Welcome to Lockwood Lightning! I'm so, so excited for this new series! Lockwood Lightning had been on my mind for years, and I just had to find the right time to fit this family saga in. I've toured many distilleries, and I'm always fascinated by the history of how each one got their start and how they've grown. I decided to add moonshine into the bourbon world for this series, so I needed strong characters to pull off each aspect.

I can't wait for you to get to know this unique family and how they all come together through the course of time and circumstances. I had to throw in a very vulnerable hero for book one, and I hope you love Nick just as much as I do! Of course, he had to have a strong shero at his side, so Silvia is exactly what he needs during this difficult time...but she's going through her own struggles.

Settle in for book one of my new series and, don't worry, books two and three are not far behind!

Happy reading,

Jules

JULES BENNETT

AN UNEXPECTED SCANDAL

HARLEQUIN
DESIRE

HARLEQUIN®
DESIRE™

Recycling programs
for this product may
not exist in your area.

ISBN-13: 978-1-335-20903-0

An Unexpected Scandal

Harlequin Enterprises ULC
22 Adelaide St. West, 40th Floor
Toronto, Ontario M5H 4E3, Canada
www.Harlequin.com

Printed in U.S.A.

USA TODAY bestselling author **Jules Bennett** has published over sixty books and never tires of writing happy endings. Writing strong heroines and alpha heroes is Jules's favorite way to spend her workdays. Jules hosts weekly contests on her Facebook fan page and loves chatting with readers on Twitter, Facebook and via email through her website. Stay up-to-date by signing up for her newsletter at julesbennett.com.

Books by Jules Bennett

Harlequin Desire

The Rancher's Heirs

Twin Secrets
Claimed by the Rancher
Taming the Texan
A Texan for Christmas

Two Brothers

Montana Seduction
California Secrets

Lockwood Lightning

An Unexpected Scandal

Visit her Author Profile page at Harlequin.com, or julesbennett.com, for more titles.

You can also find Jules Bennett on Facebook, along with other Harlequin Desire authors, at Facebook.com/harlequindesireauthors!

This book, and this entire series, is dedicated to the other half of my brain, Jessica Lemmon. I'm thankful for boat-ride plotting, FaceTime chats when we look our absolute worst and a special friendship that goes well beyond books.

One

The cool spring rain pelted Nick Campbell's back. The unopened envelope in his hand held a secret he'd yet to discover…and part of him wanted to shred it and let the secret die with his mother.

Nick stood over Lori Campbell's pearl-white casket and stared down at the spray of pink roses cascading in every direction. She had left him this letter and told him there were two more to be delivered to the others.

So many secrets, so many cryptic deathbed messages.

Honestly, he didn't care about any of that right now. The yawning ache in his heart over losing his mother trumped all other emotions.

But he'd vowed he would read the letter once she

was gone. She had passed five days ago, and he still hadn't opened it. For days he'd carried the envelope around in his pocket, thinking he'd look at it, but one thing led to another. Arrangements were made, insurance dealt with, so many details for a funeral. Nick just hadn't had the time or the energy.

Anticipation and worry gnawed at him, and he knew the moment had come. He had nothing else waiting on him, nothing pressing right this second... and he'd promised his mother.

Nick tore his eyes from the casket and gazed down at the wrinkled envelope in his hand. He tore the seal open and pulled out the letter. With a deep breath, he started to read.

Shock, anger, confusion...so many emotions rolled through him that he had nowhere to channel everything. Nick read through the letter once again, slower this time, hoping he'd read it wrong.

What the hell? How could he process her death and this, too? It was all too much to take in—and he didn't want to accept any of it.

When he'd realized his mother was indeed going to pass only a few short weeks ago, he'd closed in on himself, not wanting to even think of a future without her...let alone finishing the resort she'd started renovating with his help.

The resort that had led him to Silvia.

For one night, Silvia Lane, lead architect on the

resort project, had been more than an associate, more than an acquaintance.

She'd been passionate, giving, so damn sexy that he couldn't stop thinking about every single detail. Her hair sliding over his body, that naughty grin she'd tossed him just before she'd let her pencil dress slide down her body. And he'd never forget the way she'd cried out his name as her pleasure took over.

That heated encounter had played over and over in his mind the last four weeks. The morning after, she'd slipped back into her dress, and they'd both agreed there would be nothing beyond that night. She was new in town and building her career. She couldn't afford for anyone to know she'd slept with a client. And he sure as hell was in no position to add another complication to his life.

But she'd comforted him when grief had overtaken him. And part of him wished for more comfort from her now.

Nick's eyes scanned back over the page until the handwritten words blurred together. He wanted to shred the letter, as if that would make this entire nightmare go away. If only things could be so easy...

Unfortunately, Nick knew his mother wouldn't lie. The woman didn't have a deceitful bone in her body, and she would never purposely hurt him, not even with the bombshell she'd left him with.

That didn't mean he understood why she'd kept the truth from him for so long. Or why she'd chosen to share it with him only after she was gone and he could no longer get answers. And what had she meant about two other letters?

Nick pulled in a shaky breath and shivered against the cold rain. He'd said his private goodbyes and it was time to go. He had to move on, to continue to honor his mother's wishes, and carry out her plans.

The crunch of leaves had him jerking around, coming face-to-face with Silvia...the woman he hadn't seen since their one-night stand.

Silvia had stood back beneath the covering of a lush tree and watched as Nick clearly had a private moment over his mother's grave. He'd pulled an envelope from his pocket and studied it for some time.

Gripping her umbrella, Silvia decided she couldn't stand here forever like some stalker. She had to approach him now before she lost her nerve.

For the past five days she had tried to contact him, but then she'd learned about the death of his mother, and she knew the timing of her news couldn't be worse. She understood why he was not responding to her texts or calls.

It hadn't been because she'd broken their promise to keep it to just one night.

He was grieving, just as he'd been that night everything had changed.

She wanted to go to him, to place a hand on his

shoulder to comfort and console, but everything was different now.

They'd had a strong working relationship for the past few months, and then one night in his office, he'd broken down about his mother, and one thing led to another.

There had been attraction building since day one, when he'd hired her as the lead architect for the renovation of his mother's resort.

Being the professional she was, she had kept her erotic fantasies to herself…until that night when she hadn't.

Now look where that had landed her.

How had she fallen for his charms? It wasn't as if she hadn't been charmed by men before. Maybe it was Nick's vulnerability that night. Perhaps coupled with the impossible-to-ignore sex appeal, she'd really been fighting a losing battle.

Silvia gripped the handle of her umbrella now and shoved her other hand into her jacket pocket. The spring rain and gray skies matched her mood as she took one courageous step and then another.

Nick jerked around, his bright eyes met hers and her mind instantly flashed back to that night they'd taken their business meeting from his leather office chairs to his oversize desk…

She hadn't seen him since, but he'd always been in the forefront of her mind.

"What are you doing here?" he asked, his voice thick with emotion.

Silvia had never seen him so dressed up. He typically wore jeans and a button-down dress shirt, but now he wore a charcoal suit with matching shirt and tie. His dark blond hair perfectly styled, even in the rain, his usually scruffy jaw clean shaven.

And those glasses.

No matter the anguish he was going through, those glasses stopped her cold. She'd knocked those dark frames off his face when she'd jerked his shirt over his head that night.

Focus, Silvia. You're not here for a reunion, and he's hurting.

Neither of them could afford to get more involved than they'd been for those few hours.

He'd disappeared after, and Silvia's heart ached for him during this loss. The timing of this little secret could not be worse. She'd never lied in her life and she certainly wasn't about to start now, not even to save him from more shocking news.

"I'm checking on you," she told him honestly. "I didn't want to smother you during the service. I saw so many people, and I just… I don't really belong here, but I had to come."

Understatement.

"I called and texted," she went on as the rain continued to pelt her umbrella. "I figured this was the only place we could talk."

Droplets clung to his darkened hair, normally a dirty blond when dry. He seemed oblivious to the fact that he stood before her absolutely soaked, with raindrops dotting his lenses.

He still looked too damn good.

"Talk?" Nick shook his head and removed his glasses. He wiped a hand down his face, flinging the moisture aside. "Work is going to have to wait. I know I was pushing for this project to be done, but—"

"I'm not here about work."

His eyes widened for a split second before his lips thinned. "We can talk in the car."

Guilt tugged at her. He stood at his mother's casket, saying his final goodbyes, and here she was, demanding they talk.

If her news weren't so life changing, she wouldn't be here.

"I can go wait in my car," she told him, then nodded toward the casket. "You take your time."

She turned and walked away, not giving him a chance to argue or ask questions. She'd told him they had to talk, and he'd agreed—now she and her bundle of nerves just had to go and keep each other company until he joined them.

The moment she slid behind the wheel, Silvia closed her eyes and willed herself to remain calm. Getting worked up would not change the circumstances, and she had to maintain control. Getting emotional or hysterical wouldn't help and she prided herself on being professional. Now that her professional life had rolled into her personal life, she still had to maintain her composure.

Silvia had only been in her car a couple minutes when the passenger door opened and Nick leaned in.

"I'm soaking wet. Just follow me back to my place. I'll change and we can talk."

He slammed the door before she could say a word, and Silvia dropped her head back against the headrest. She'd followed him here in the rain for a number of reasons. She didn't want to go to his house, didn't want to be on his turf when she broke the news, and she didn't want to wait.

So she didn't.

Silvia opened her car door and stepped out, sans umbrella. She jerked the knot on her trench coat and marched toward Nick's menacing black SUV. Nerves and fear swirled together, but she swallowed back the emotions to focus on the task.

"I need to talk now," she demanded to his back.

He turned, clearly stunned that she had not obeyed his command to just follow him home. But she was done waiting and keeping this secret to herself. She always tackled issues head on, and she was ready to start planning the inevitable changes that were to come.

There was no right time to say it, so she just said it.

"I'm pregnant."

Nick slowly turned all the way around to face her, his eyes never wavering. Silvia practically held her breath, waiting on him to say something or have some reaction other than a blank stare.

"Nick?" she finally said.

"Meet me at my house."

And with that he turned, got into his truck and drove off. Looked like she would be following him to his house after all, but the first order of business would be teaching Nick Campbell that she didn't take commands from anyone.

Two

If this day could get any worse, Nick sure as hell didn't want to know how.

First, he laid his mother to rest.

Second, he'd read the final words of his mother in the form of a letter that had left him reeling and shaken.

And finally…this was the real kick in the gut. The lead architect on his mother's multi-million-dollar resort and the only woman he'd ever had a one-night stand with informed him she was pregnant.

He pulled up the long, curvy drive leading to his private mountain home overlooking the Great Smoky Mountains National Park. The tall red spruce and Fraser firs flanked each side of the drive and he'd been sure to leave as many untouched as possible when he'd cleared his lot for his three-story cabin.

This place had always been a tranquil escape from his hectic life and travel as a business mogul and investor. But now, even the sight of the cozy stone home that he'd had built only a few years ago didn't calm him. His nerves were all over the place, coupled with guilt and pain.

A child.

He was going to be a father? Supposedly, anyway. He knew nothing about parenting. He'd never even wanted a family.

For nearly forty years, he'd wondered who his own father was, but his mother had always said he was better off not knowing. How ironic that now he was sliding into a role he knew absolutely nothing about.

And to become a parent with a woman he had only been intimate with once?

Oh, he'd fantasized about her plenty before that night. Her quick wit and smart business sense had been total turn-ons, not to mention they meshed perfectly together while working on the designs for the mountain resort he would be opening in the fall.

Even his mother had adored Silvia.

Those two had laughed and really seemed to be on the same page when it came to the minute details of the elite, yet cozy mountain getaway. Nick had loved seeing his mother so happy in her final days, but from his vantage point, having Silvia penetrate another layer of his life wasn't smart. A quick fling was one thing, but getting too personal, too permanent, could be a disaster.

Clearly they were entering dangerous territory if he was indeed the father of her child. And, honestly, he didn't believe she would lie about this. He trusted Silvia or she wouldn't be on this project... and he wouldn't have slept with her.

Nick pulled into his garage and left the door open for Silvia to follow. He had no clue what to say. Hell, on a good day he wouldn't know how to react to the news that he was going to be a daddy, but today he was emotionally drained and had nothing left to give.

He stepped from his SUV and removed his suit jacket, then unbuttoned the top two buttons of his dress shirt before rolling up the sleeves. Damn thing was too confining. He certainly wasn't a suit type of guy on a normal day.

His cell vibrated in his pocket, and he pulled the phone out, only to ignore the caller. Rusty Lockwood's office. Of course they'd call *now*, when Nick's world seemed to be falling apart.

He had been demanding a meeting for weeks.

Rusty had been the proverbial thorn in Nick's side for far too long, and today was not the day to deal with that mess. The moonshine mogul and CEO of Lockwood Lightning ruled the resorts and bars of this upscale area with an iron fist. You served Lockwood moonshine or you served nothing at all. Anyone who refused to bow down to Rusty didn't receive a liquor license. And since the grade-A bastard had refused the liquor license for Nick's mom's resort, Rusty was also Nick's main nemesis.

One crisis at a time.

He turned back to Silvia to take care of the current, more pressing crisis.

"I tell you I am pregnant and you just drive off?" Silvia stated as she stepped into the garage and smoothed her wet hair from her face.

"Did you want to get into this at the cemetery?" he countered, the fear and uncertainty raging inside of him.

When she only stared, Nick turned and headed inside—again, he left the door open for her to follow. He heard the most unladylike growl behind him and cursed beneath his breath. He was being an ass, and she didn't deserve it. His emotions were all over the place and he had to take a deep breath and get himself under control.

It wasn't until she'd stepped into the kitchen that Nick realized she'd gotten completely soaked from the downpour. He was soaked, too, but he'd been numb most of the day anyway. She shouldn't have to be miserable.

"I'll grab us some towels," he muttered as he headed down the short hallway toward one of the guest baths.

Nick also grabbed the thick white robe off the back of the door and turned to find Silvia standing in the doorway.

"Are you running from me?" she asked, blocking his exit and holding his gaze.

He handed over the towel and the robe. "I'm not running," he corrected. "I'm trying to get us dry."

And maybe he needed to stay busy to ignore all the emotions he wasn't ready to face.

Silvia clutched the items in her hands and continued to stare at him. Even with her hair hanging in ropelike dark crimson strands, her wet clothes plastered to her shapely form and her face void of most makeup, she was still a damn knockout.

He'd often wondered how he would feel when he saw her again after that night. Now he knew. Even with everything going on, he wanted her. Apparently, nothing could diminish the pull between them.

"I'm not purposely being a jerk," he started as he raked the towel over his head. "I'm just… Hell, I don't even know what to say."

"I'm not sure what can be said at this point." Silvia patted her face and squeezed her hair with the towel. "I tried getting in touch with you, but you were busy with your mother. I hated showing up at the cemetery, but I knew I would find you there. I purposely waited until everyone else was gone."

In the pouring rain, she'd waited. He'd never met anyone as determined as she was.

"I just want you to know that I don't expect anything of you," she went on. "I mean, if you want to be part of our lives, that's up to you, but I'm not trapping you and I'm not—"

"Stop."

Nick dropped his towel to the floor and reached for hers. She had draped the robe over her arm, but water still dripped from her hair, droplets clinging to her light lashes. Those bright blue eyes remained locked on him as he took her towel and dried her hair. His body reacted, as it always did when she was around, but somehow, knowing she was carrying his child only made him crave her more.

He stepped back because his emotions were too raw, too intense.

"My mother raised me by herself." Nick handed her the towel and watched her slide it down the darkened red strands. "She struggled, sometimes working two jobs, but she never missed my ball games and was always my biggest cheerleader. I never felt like I lacked a father. She was an amazing woman."

Speaking of her in the past tense seemed so strange, so painful…so foreign. She should still be here, alive and vibrant, and finalizing plans on the Smoky Mountains resort she'd always dreamed of opening. And how would she have reacted to the possibility of being a grandmother?

Nick swallowed and went on. "As I got older, I appreciated her drive and determination. That's why I'm so successful today."

"Are you bragging?" Silvia asked, her mouth kicking up in a slight grin.

"Stating facts," he corrected. "What I'm saying is that my mother was a kick-ass woman, and I believe you're just as stubborn and driven."

Silvia blinked. "Um…thanks?"

"Listen, you won't be doing this alone." Nick stepped closer again and gripped her shoulders. "I know what it's like to grow up without a father, but this child will not."

He waited for her to say something, to argue or thank him…hell, he didn't know what to expect. None of this was familiar territory, but he never backed down from a responsibility, and he sure as hell wasn't going to start now with the most important role of his life.

He might not know what it was to have a good father, but he'd try his damnedest to be one.

After that night, when they'd both claimed it was a mistake, neither of them had wanted anyone to know what had taken place in private. Now, though, keeping that secret would be impossible. He couldn't stand by her side without people noticing.

"I want you to have as much of a role as you want," she told him. "But I have to put the needs and the security of the baby first. So if you're going to be around for a little bit and then shirk your daddy duties, I'd rather you not be around at all."

Shirk his duties? Not likely. Clearly she didn't know him very well.

"I'm not going anywhere," he assured her.

She might not believe him, she might have her doubts, but he'd show her with his actions. This child would never question where his or her father was. Nick would always be present and available. Never before had he even thought to put something or someone ahead of his work, but from this moment on, his baby would come first.

Even though his world had seemed to come to a halt with losing his mother, the fact was, Silvia's had kept going and she'd been holding this in until they could speak.

"How are you feeling?" he asked, truly wanting to know how she felt.

Silvia jerked as if the question stunned her. "Oh, well, fine, I guess. I mean, I'm tired, but that's normal, from what I've read. I don't have morning sickness, so I hope that doesn't happen."

She looked amazing. Not a dark circle, not a pale complexion…nothing. Silvia Lane epitomized class and beauty, even when soaking wet and dealing with an unexpected pregnancy.

And if not for a moment of weakness and a few gin and tonics with extra lime, this sexy architect might not have given a rough country boy like him the time of day. Oh, he had money—more than he would ever know what to do with—but that didn't change his roots, a mountain childhood with a struggling single mom.

Silvia was the total opposite with her polished

look and her Ivy League degrees. Her background was likely full of cotillions and dinner parties while his had been frozen dinners in front of the television.

"What was that letter I saw you with earlier?"

Her question pulled him back. "What?"

"At the cemetery," she added. "You were reading a letter, and you seemed, I don't know, angry or hurt. Both."

Hurt? Yeah, that he hadn't been told the truth before his mother passed away.

He'd read the letter twice and already had the damn thing memorized. There was no way he could ever forget his mother's final words, her final confession. The one that would forever alter his life from this moment forward.

Nick,

I'm sorry I couldn't tell you this while I was alive. Maybe I'm a coward, but I just wanted to spare you the pain of the truth for as long as possible. Now, though, I want you to have all of the information available to move forward. You're the smartest, bravest person I know, and I trust you will continue to do the right thing.

For years you asked about your father, and I never wanted you to know the truth. With me gone, you deserve to know everything, even if it's not what you expected or what you want

*to hear. I hope you don't hate me, and I hope
you don't think badly of me.*

Rusty Lockwood is your biological father.

Nick despised the man. He had been butting heads
with the arrogant prick for the past year. Everyone
in Tennessee knew who Rusty Lockwood was and
how conniving he was in business. His moonshine
distillery drew in thousands of tourists a year, but
Rusty was always under the microscope and dodg-
ing rumors of illegal actions.

Nick would bet his private jet that the man didn't
have one truly loyal friend. Rusty was as crooked and
as underhanded as they came. His millions stemmed
from distributing backwoods moonshine long before
the white lightning was legal. He'd only kept his head
above water because he had certain politicians and
the city council in his back pocket.

And now he was the power behind this place. Nick
refused to let this go on any longer than necessary.
Rusty had to be stopped.

How the hell had Nick's mother gotten mixed up
with Rusty Lockwood to begin with? Had he used
her and discarded her? Had they actually had a relationship?

Nick recalled the final portion of the letter.

*I know this is a shock to you, but I'm tell-
ing you the truth. I wish I could tell you your
father was anyone else, but I can't. I just want*

*you to be careful. He's vicious, but I can't say
I regret my past because it gave me you.*

*He paid me fifty thousand dollars when
I told him about you. He gave me money to
leave him alone and keep his name off the
birth certificate. I'm not ashamed I took the
money—that's how I was able to buy us that
small home.*

*I found out over the years that he fathered
two other sons. I'm pretty sure he knows nothing about them, and I hope you all find your
way to each other. I've sent them letters as
well, and what they decide to do will ultimately
be up to them. Continue making me proud. Get
my resort up and running. I wouldn't trust anyone else to that task.*

I'll love you even in death, Nick. Stay safe.

Nick pulled himself back to the moment. Silvia
stared at him, still waiting on an answer.

"It was nothing," he lied.

Because the life Nick had known before this day
was gone. Now he had choices to make as his past
and his future collided.

Three

"And don't forget to have that to me by the end of the day," Clark said with a wink. "You don't want to mess up your six-month probationary period when you're so close to the end."

Silvia stared at the doorway long after her boss slunk away. Every time he winked that damn wink, she expected an air gun with his hand. And that snarky laugh grated on her every nerve. But she was still fairly new to Green Valley, Tennessee, and she needed this job. She'd moved here from Charlotte, wanting to be closer to the mountains she'd always visited as a child. Why not live in the most peaceful place she could think of?

Granted she wasn't feeling much peace right now.

Clark wasn't her favorite person, not by any means, but this firm was the best in all of Tennessee, so she was thankful for the position. Not to mention she was the only woman in the entire office; even the assistants and the interns were male. She liked to think that said something about her work ethic and her killer skills, but who knew. They likely were worried about a lawsuit, so they needed a woman to prove they were inclusive.

Silvia hadn't yet told her boss that she was expecting. Since the pregnancy was still early, and she hadn't finished the probationary period he'd tried to joke about, she didn't see the need—plus, she didn't think her personal life was any of his business...yet.

She hadn't seen Nick since she'd spoken to him yesterday after his mother's funeral. He'd looked so lost, so stricken with grief, but she couldn't keep the baby a secret from him.

She wouldn't.

She also couldn't turn off her damn hormones where he was concerned. The way he'd gently dried her hair really shouldn't have turned her on, but her body had responded just the same as when he'd taken her on his desk in his office a month ago.

As if she needed another reason to feel a pull toward the man who'd given her the best sexual experience of her life.

That whole rugged, I-don't-give-a-damn attitude really turned her on in ways she couldn't explain.

And the glasses, she couldn't forget those. He didn't wear them all the time, but when he did…

Maybe she was tired of proving herself to men like her boss. Maybe the way Nick actually valued her opinion was refreshing. He listened to her, he'd sought her out for this particular project and she could tell that he hadn't been wanting to get in her pants from the get-go. He'd always treated her with respect.

Or maybe she'd just had enough of controlling her emotions, and when he had let that twinge of vulnerability show in his office that night, she'd taken advantage. She'd taken what she wanted.

Now she was pregnant.

Her one and only one-night stand, the one time she'd let herself bend the rules just a bit, and her life was altered forever.

But she didn't have regrets. Regretting any situation wouldn't change the outcome, and regrets always meant looking in the past. She didn't have time for that.

Silvia came to her feet and circled her desk in her tiny office with no window. That was definitely one of her next goals in this building was to secure a window view. It seemed such a shame to work in such a picturesque place and have no view of the mountains.

After flicking the lock into place—because she didn't want anyone barging in while she was making an appointment with an obstetrician—Silvia pulled out her cell.

Her hands shook. While she frequently made regular doctor's appointments, she'd never made a call like this.

Sleeping with a client was a serious no-no, especially for a newbie to the firm like her. But getting pregnant? Silvia had yet to find that chapter in the company handbook.

But she would remain professional about all of this—she had to. Having been raised in foster care, Silvia had always felt like she had to work harder to measure up, to prove herself. Maybe that was all in her own mind, but the self-imposed pressure to do her best at all times was all she'd ever known.

Moments later, Silvia's appointment was made, and she felt a little more in control of this situation. As much as she would love the fun of going online and making a Pinterest board or searching for the perfect maternity clothes and best baby must-haves, she still had a demanding job to do.

Graduating at the top of her class from Cornell University meant she could manipulate design plans in her sleep and construct a draft like a champ. But for this situation, she just didn't know what steps to take next. Given her upbringing, or lack thereof, she had to be cautious and ensure each decision worked for the good of her child. Bouncing around from foster home to foster home had taught her so much—life's lessons learned the hard way.

She wanted an easier life for her child. She wanted

the stability that she'd never had. She wanted her baby to enjoy being a kid and not worry about where he or she would lay their head at night or if mommy and daddy loved them.

Shaking away some not-so-pleasant memories, Silvia glanced to her computer and stared at Nick's name highlighted in yellow for their on-site meeting this afternoon. She hadn't forgotten about it, but they hadn't discussed getting together when she'd seen him yesterday. Would he want to reschedule? He'd just laid his mother to rest and found out he was going to be a father. Jumping back into work seemed a bit soon, didn't it?

No, someone like Nick would want to push forward. He had started this particular project in honor of his mother. Her dream had always been to own a posh mountain resort, and Nick was making every bit of that dream happen—with Silvia's help.

Silvia had absolutely loved Lori Campbell. The woman had been in poor health by the time Silvia entered the picture, but Lori had still insisted on coming to as many design meetings as possible. A few were even done via video conference so she could attend and continue to give her input. Lori had been a determined woman, and Silvia could appreciate that. She respected Lori so much for going after what she wanted, even as a single mother who had clearly worked hard to give her only son a successful life.

She had always been serious a go-getter, or Nick would not have turned out so headstrong and driven.

After their one-night stand, Silvia had worried about how she and Nick would continue their working relationship. She'd never slept with a colleague or a client, and this job was her step up. She'd worked hard to become an architect and had taken a risk moving to a place where she knew nobody.

And now there was so much more to consider.

Like the fact that seeing him again had only reminded her that their one passionate night had definitely not been enough.

Nick pulled his work truck into the site and killed the engine. It had taken all of his willpower not to cancel his meeting with Silvia so he could confront Rusty Lockwood.

But this bit of shocking news would take some time to process. He needed to formulate a flawless, effective plan. With this news, Nick suddenly had an edge up on Russ, which was exactly the way he wanted, no needed, to keep things.

Before this, they'd been butting heads over a liquor license issue, but not even Russ's dirty hands in the pockets of the city council would stop Nick from pursuing what he needed for his resort. He owed his mother.

Besides, he loathed people like Rusty, who bullied simply because they had the power and the money.

Someone needed to take Rusty down, and Nick did not mind being the one to step up to the plate.

Even so, barging into Rusty's office with his life-altering news now would only be a mistake.

He could put this information to better use.

And he'd be talking to Rusty soon enough. Through some scouring, Nick had discovered there was a poker game between local bigwigs that took place in the back room at the Rogue Wingman bar every Friday night. Nick had instantly taken an interest in the game. Rusty would be there, and so would Nick.

A flash of red hair caught his eye, and Nick watched through the windshield as Silvia walked out of the front door of the old, historic building. She had on a black jumpsuit that she probably deemed professional, but it just looked sexy as hell to him. With all of that red hair hanging down her back in a mass of waves…

Yeah, one night definitely hadn't been enough if he was still fantasizing about how those silky strands felt across his skin.

She stared up at the building and shielded the late-spring sun from her eyes with her hand. The wind tossed around her curls as she continued to study the area.

Nick had no clue how to shift from lover to coworker—to father—but he better get used to all of that, because now he owned all the hats.

Instead of sitting there like a creeper, Nick exited

the truck and pocketed his phone. Despite the turmoil that his life had become—the discovery of a supposed father, possibly some half brothers, his own impending parenthood and a woman he couldn't seem to forget—Nick would see this project through. At least this resort was one damn thing he could control.

His mother had worked at some of the finest establishments across the nation, but she'd landed in Tennessee as a maid at a local hotel. No matter how poor they were or how they struggled to make ends meet, his mother always valued her job and worked her ass off. She used to tell him about her dream of being able to afford to stay in an elegant place where she could order room service and watch the sun rise over the mountains.

She had the simplest of goals, and Nick had wanted her to live long enough to see this historic building transformed into her dream.

She'd never see it, but he'd build it for her anyway.

Before Nick reached Silvia, she'd disappeared back inside. He hadn't been to the site in a few weeks, what with his mom's declining health and then the funeral arrangements. He was anxious to see the progress and get back to some semblance of normal…or at least figure out his new normal.

The moment he stepped through the old double wooden doors, his breath caught in his throat. Maybe there wasn't so much progress as there was destruction. The place had been stripped down, and piles of rubble lay here and there. The wide, curved staircase proudly stood directly ahead—that was one of the main things Lori hadn't wanted touched other than to refinish it to its original state. Between the location of the building, which was perched on top of one of the Great Smoky Mountains, and the grand staircase, Lori had fallen in love with the place the first time Nick brought her here. He had to admit, he had fallen in love himself. This was the perfect location for an upscale getaway with a million-dollar view.

A muttered curse from behind the stairs had Nick watching his step as he made his way over the roughened wood floors.

"Silvia?"

"Back here," she called.

Nick followed the string of curses until he found her, and he quickly realized her problem. That sexy jumpsuit had just gotten even sexier with a rip down the side, exposing a red strap that no doubt belonged to a thong…if his memory served him correctly, that was her favorite style of underwear. He could fully admit he was a fan himself.

But then he noticed a nasty scratch on her hip. Nick stepped over the pile of rough boards to close the distance between them.

"I just took the tag off this outfit," she grumbled, attempting to hold the two pieces together like that would solve her problems.

"Let me see." He swatted her hands away until

the fabric hung around the wound. "How did you do this?"

Nick bent down to examine how deep the cut was.

"The edge of that pile over there. I looked right at it and still managed to snag a corner."

Nick straightened and met her bright eyes. "And you're not wearing your hard hat."

She laughed, crossing her arms over her chest. "Yours is a pretty shade of…oh, wait. You're not wearing one, either."

Nick didn't want to get into an argument—he seriously didn't have the energy today. How could he keep her safe when she volleyed comebacks that were so on point?

And it was that damn strong-will that had first attracted him. Now he didn't find it so sexy when he was the target of her stubbornness.

"I haven't been here in weeks, so I didn't know there was such destruction," he defended. "You knew better."

Silvia shook her head. "Relax. My hard hat is over there with my stuff, and the crew isn't coming in until later. I do know how to do my job."

"Then put on the hat."

"Because that would have saved my leg from being scratched?" she threw back. "Listen, maybe we should reschedule this meeting. You've got so much going on—"

"No."

He wasn't rescheduling, and he was not going to let her tell him what he needed. He needed to work, damn it. He needed to get some regularity back in his life, and this was the only area he currently had control over.

After so many years living in poverty with his mother, he'd finally made it. With his career as an investor and renovator, he had made a name for himself, and he was damn good at what he did. He worked at something he could be proud of.

His personal life? That was something he was going to have to work on…starting with the woman carrying his child.

"Nobody would think anything if you took time off," she added, her voice softening.

He hated pity. He'd had that soul-sucking emotion thrown out at him as a child, and he'd come too far to revert back to it now. Pity for being the poor, hillbilly kid with clothes that had seen better days. Pity for not having a dad. He'd pushed through that web of pity. It had held him down for years. Until he'd gone to college on a baseball scholarship, earned a degree in half the time, and made wise investments before turning all that money around to help others. Determination and drive made all the difference.

It would make the difference now, too.

"I had time off," he reminded her. "My mother would want me to move on and see this through."

When Silvia opened her mouth, he went on. "Get

the hard hat on. Better yet, we shouldn't be meeting here, not in your condition. I can wait on the foreman to arrive if you'd like to get back to the office."

Something Nick didn't recognize swept over her features as she squared her shoulders and tipped up her chin.

Well, hell. He didn't know what he'd said that had pissed her off, but he had a feeling he was about to find out.

Four

If Nick Campbell thought for one second that she would be a pushover or let him rule her every move simply because she was pregnant with his child, he was a damn idiot. But, because she was feeling generous and knew he was going through a difficult time, she opted not to throat punch him.

"My office is where I do creative work," she started. "My office is also where I sometimes meet clients for the first time or answer emails. But when I schedule an on-site meeting, I tend to need to go to the actual site. You never had an issue working with me on this project before."

"You weren't carrying my baby before."

Silvia ignored her instinct to think his statement

was sweet in some new-dad-worry kind of way and tried to figure out how to shut down this conversation. She didn't want them talking so openly about this. Anyone could walk in and hear, and she needed to keep her pregnancy—and her intimacy with Nick—a secret for now.

She'd worked too hard for her current position to be unprofessional now. And sleeping with a client was the furthest thing from professional she could think of.

Still, that had honestly been the most passionate, hottest night of her life. She'd let her guard down one time, allowed herself to enjoy the hell out him, and now her whole life had shifted. Not only did she have to find a way to prove she was the best at her job, she also had to figure out how to make it all work with being a mother.

"I am still more than capable of working," she countered. "If you're worried about my health, maybe you shouldn't purposely be trying to piss me off. You're raising my blood pressure."

Nick's lips twitched, but he said nothing as he turned on his heel and crossed over to her things, which she'd set on a pile of boards. He grabbed the hard hat, came back, and plopped it down on her head.

"Now, tell me what's been going on the past few weeks."

Damn it. She wanted to be irritated at him for attempting to tell her what to do, but he didn't continue arguing to get his point across. Nick was definitely more a man of action than words.

It was those actions that she kept replaying over and over in her mind.

He'd been fair to his workers, and went out of his way to be kind. That was the sign of a true leader.

But the way he'd looked at her with desire during the beginning stages of this project, yet still managed to be professional had completely turned her on in ways she still couldn't explain. She still couldn't quite get her footing where her need for Nick was concerned.

How could one night of passion have such an impact? How could she still want him despite everything? They'd both agreed it wouldn't go further than one night, but now she had a child to consider. There wouldn't be any grand gestures of romance from either of them. They both had very lucrative careers they were married to and past baggage. Didn't everyone have a load of baggage? Well, she wasn't in the mindset to take on anyone else's…no matter how much she wanted him.

"As you can see, the entire lobby area has been gutted, but we are resurfacing the old hardwoods and keeping the copper ceiling." She gripped the gaping material at her thigh. "You requested we keep as much as possible and restore it, so all of the old trim is being housed in the basement for now and will be cleaned up and put back in place."

Silvia continued to go over what had been done in the past couple of weeks, plus the next steps. All the while, Nick kept those striking dark blue eyes on her.

If she thought he'd been potent before they'd slept together, that was nothing compared to now. She knew the intensity of those eyes during moments of pleasure—she vividly recalled how her body shivered as he raked that hungry gaze over her. She was shivering a little even now remembering how that same gaze traveled over her bare skin.

"Silvia?"

His low voice jerked her back, and she realized she had stopped talking and she'd been staring... remembering.

Great. Just what she didn't need—to lose touch with what was important here, and it wasn't her desires. Nick trusted her with this project. He'd chosen her because he trusted her work, and because she was a woman and he wanted someone who could relate to his mother's vision. There was pressure to get this right. Added to that, several coworkers at her firm were just waiting on her to fail so they could swoop in and save the day...and gain the healthy paycheck that came from working with world-renowned mogul Nick Campbell.

Silvia had to honor the vow she'd made to herself way back in foster care—she would always rely only on herself and rise above any obstacle. She wouldn't depend on anyone to hold her up or escort her through life. And she wasn't going to start now. She refused to rely on Nick, not financially and not emotionally.

Just because she kept thinking back to their night together and fantasizing didn't mean it could happen again.

"As I was saying," she went on, clearing her throat.

"I remember, too."

Silvia stilled. Her heart thumped heavily; her hand gripped the torn material even tighter. His low tone washed over her, thrusting her back to that night when he'd whispered sultry words in the dark.

"I recognize fantasizing," he added, taking a step forward, his eyes never wavering from hers.

Silvia didn't back up—she refused to seem weak or intimidated, because she already looked absurd standing here in a hard hat and a torn jumpsuit.

"Who says I was daydreaming?" she asked, cursing herself when her voice cracked.

Nick settled his hand on her hip and stared down into her eyes. He made her feel almost…well, protected. She'd never felt completely protected in her life, and she was not going to let herself get comfortable with the feeling now. All the years of taking care of herself had hopefully prepared her for the next role she would take on as mother and provider.

She couldn't add lover or girlfriend or anything else to the mix. Getting swept up in hormones would not benefit anyone long-term.

"You don't have to say a word," he murmured as he leaned in closer. "Your face is full of expressions... and I recall each and every one from our night together."

Silvia's body heated with his words, his delicate touch, his nearness. She placed a hand on his chest and stared into those mesmerizing eyes.

"We're having a baby," she reminded him. "Everything has changed. But still, we can't do this again."

"Why not?" he countered. "The desire hasn't gone away."

He inched forward, his lips merely a breath away. Her body ached for him to touch her, to prove to her that everything she recalled was real and perfect.

Why couldn't they do this again? She was having a difficult time remembering with him standing so close.

The slam of a truck door pulled Silvia back. She jerked away as reality smacked her in the face.

"Because we're working together," she stated, reminding herself. "This is my first project with a new firm. I can't afford to get tangled with a client."

Something harsh washed over his face. "Too late."

He barely got the words out before the foreman for the project came strolling in wearing his hard hat, work boots, and denim overalls. Silvia gripped the material together at her thigh and skirted around Nick. She had to remain in control of this situation, of her emotions, or she'd find herself right back where she'd been a month ago.

Naked and in his arms begging for more.

Nick stared at the jewelry on the desk in his home office. He'd requested that his mother's jewelry be returned after the funeral, and his assistant had just dropped the pieces off earlier.

Propping his hands on his hips, he contemplated what to do with them. His mother had always worn the plain diamond necklace. It was the smallest stone in the simplest of settings, but that's what Nick had purchased for her with his first check. He had wanted her to have something nice after all the years of working so hard to take care of him.

As he'd become more successful, he'd tried to get her to choose a new necklace or at least take this one off. She deserved better, bigger, but she'd said over and over that this necklace meant more to her than any other ever would and she didn't want to replace it.

He didn't think the simple gold hoops were worth anything, but she'd always worn them, too.

So now Nick stood in his home office and stared at the last few items of his mother's. Well, and the letter that he had locked away in his safe.

After leaving Silvia at the site earlier, he had driven around, trying to put his thoughts into some nice, neat order, but considering his entire life was in chaos, there was no way to organize his thoughts.

Ultimately, he'd ended up at home. He probably should go in to the office, but there wasn't a thing he couldn't do from home, and he wasn't quite ready to hear the condolences or be on the receiving end of countless hugs. He knew his employees meant well—they had showered him with food, flowers, cards—but he just couldn't see them face-to-face right now.

When his assistant had brought the jewelry, he'd also informed Nick that they had been denied once again for the hard liquor license for the new resort. Not that Nick had believed it would pass for him when it hadn't for others in the area, but he wished he had at least one break right now.

Regardless of all the changes in his life, he wouldn't back down. Rusty Lockwood might think he ran the town and had all the power, but Nick had his own leverage right now. Rusty had no idea about the damning letter left behind revealing the truth.

Would Rusty even care that he had a son? Would he be interested in knowing that there might be others who would come forward?

Nick planned to keep the information guarded until it was time to strike. He wanted to cause the worst possible blow to Rusty Lockwood. That man needed to be knocked down several proverbial pegs. The fact that he continued to monopolize the local liquor world was beyond absurd.

Green Valley and the surrounding areas were rich with moonshine history. The stories of how "white lightning" was once sold illegally until the state realized what an investment it would be to legalize the drink. Tourists traveled from all over the globe for tastings and to experience the atmosphere and beauty of the Great Smoky Mountains.

Nick understood wanting to capitalize on the market, but Rusty couldn't just keep his iron fist clutched around the entire industry.

There was no way Nick would open a resort and not serve hard liquor. A glass of bourbon or even a shot of moonshine was perfectly acceptable, and most definitely expected, in this area. Nick had every intention of making this upscale getaway top notch, high class and every single thing his mother envisioned. He wouldn't let one man with too much power rule over him. There was too much at stake and he'd made his mother a promise he fully intended to keep.

Nick took the small velvet pouch and slid the jewelry back inside then took everything over to his safe, which was behind a section of books in a built-in bookcase. As he opened the safe, his eyes landed on the letter, the envelope crumpled around the edges.

The initial anger and confusion had lessened, replaced by curiosity and worry. His mother had kept such a life-altering secret for decades. Not only regarding the identity of Nick's biological father, but also the fact there were two half brothers out there somewhere.

Were they also guys he knew? Were they in Green Valley, Tennessee? Nick had so many questions, but he would have to have patience. Time would reveal all the answers.

To know that his mother had carried this secret around for so long, plus that she'd gone above and beyond to make sure she provided his every need, humbled Nick. The love that she'd expressed without words, just to try to keep him safe and protected because she truly believed Rusty to be a monster. Likely Rusty would've tried to use his paternity as some type of blackmail if he could have figured out a way to gain anything further for himself.

Nick's mother had been strong—stronger than he'd realized until now.

Which reminded him of another strong woman.

Silvia would do anything for her child, of that he was certain. She'd told him the truth, but she'd also been pushing him away. She would insist on doing everything on her own, simply to prove she could, but he didn't want her to ever for a second feel like she was in this alone. Everyone needed a shoulder to lean on at some point.

Nick knew without a doubt that Silvia would never ask for help or admit that she needed him. That was fine. Her pride and her independence were just two of the qualities he had originally found so damn attractive. Her sexy little suits didn't hurt, either.

Pushing aside his past and focusing on the present, Nick shut the safe and arranged the books back in place. He could mourn and focus on everything that had happened with his mother's death, with the secrets she'd kept, or he could take hold of this information and honor his mother's reasons for protecting him. She'd done what she'd thought was right under the circumstances, and now she'd given him the truth as her final gift.

Nick's cell vibrated on his desk, and he glanced over his shoulder to see Silvia's name.

In two quick steps, he crossed and answered.

"Silvia."

"I'm at your gate," she stated. "Let me in."

Demanding women had never appealed to him before, but damn, this one did. He'd have to tell her about the bell to ring on the keypad that would alert him she was here.

Nick disconnected the call and made a quick tap on his app that unlocked the wrought iron gate at the bottom of the mountain. Nick didn't know what warranted her coming back to his house, but he was certainly not going to complain.

Nick went to the front of the house and waited on the covered porch. He hadn't realized it had started raining while he'd been home, but the darkened skies made it look as if they were in for one hell of a spring storm.

The weather seemed to be a metaphor for his life as of late.

Silvia brought her car to a stop in the curve of the drive closest to the porch steps. The rain pelted the vehicle, and she reached toward the passenger floorboard to see where her umbrella had gone. Those things were never close when she needed them, and lately she had needed them more than usual. Crazy spring weather.

Cursing, she realized she'd just have to run to the porch and become a haggard, wet mess…pretty much just like the last time she was here.

Silvia turned to reach for her handle and screamed.

One second ago Nick had been on his porch, but now he stood at her door with an umbrella, being all southern gentleman and making that speech she rehearsed vanish.

Damn him for being so considerate. Those kind little gestures were definitely not helping her self-control. At least he wasn't wearing his glasses right now. The look of him in those things was pretty much a panty dropper, and she seriously needed to keep those in place.

Nick reached for the handle and opened the door, making sure to hold the umbrella over the opening as she got out.

"Seems to be a theme lately," he told her with a sexy, cockeyed grin.

"I'm not staying long."

She made the statement more for herself than for him, but he merely widened his smile and hooked an arm around her waist. As he led her to the porch, she huddled against his side away from the pelting rain… and instantly knew coming here was a mistake.

She'd wanted to talk face-to-face, to lay down some boundaries about workplace etiquette and how they needed to keep their personal relationship separate from their business one. And by personal, she meant the baby…not the attraction that she needed to ignore and put in the past.

Once on the porch, Nick shook out the umbrella and propped it next to a stone column. Nick's house was exactly like him: bold, masculine and magnificent. Situated up on the mountainside, the place offered spectacular views, even better than her own mountain home only ten minutes away. But he didn't know where she lived, and for now she wanted to keep it that way.

There had to be some division between personal and professional until they had a good foundation for moving forward with this baby bond they'd share forever. She had to curb the attraction until she was positive the future of her child was secure.

"Have you had dinner?" he asked.

Silvia shook her head. "No, but I'm not here for that. I won't be long."

"Well, I'm hungry." He turned and opened the massive wooden door. "You can talk while I cook. If you're still talking when it's done, you might as well stay."

She stared at him, but he extended his arm in a silent gesture for her to come in. Silvia let out a sigh and marched past him. She wasn't staying for dinner…she *wasn't*. Was he purposely trying to seduce her?

Yet again, a man of action.

Without a word, Nick started toward the back of the house and into the kitchen. Silvia set her purse on the table inside the door and followed. There. Her keys and her phone were close to the door through which she would be exiting very, very soon.

Silvia stepped into the kitchen and barely contained a gasp. The entire back wall was one breathtaking view, with sliding glass doors that opened to the most magnificent patio. Even in the rain and under the darkening skies, she could make out a tiered eating area and pool.

This design was most definitely an architect's dream. She wanted to explore further.

"Go ahead and open it up," he told her as he pulled out a round baking stone and set it on the concrete center island. "I love listening to the rain. Thunder and lightning have always fascinated me."

Silvia made her way across the spacious room and slid open first one door and then the other. The refreshing aroma of the rain hit her, and she pulled in a deep breath. There was something so calming about the crisp mountain air. It was nearly impossible to be in a bad mood or let worries consume her.

She'd come to Green Valley for the serenity that only the Smoky Mountains could offer. Visiting a handful of times a year simply hadn't been enough. She wanted to settle here and now that she was expecting, she couldn't think of a better place to raise her child.

"I'm making my famous barbecue chicken pizza," he told her. "The dough has been rising since this morning."

Silvia jerked her head around, fully expecting him to be smirking at her or laughing at the joke, but no. Nick wasn't even looking her way as he worked the dough with his hands, and within moments, he was tossing it up in the air and catching it like a pro. The dough naturally stretched with each fling.

"You make your own pizza dough?" she asked, still stunned. What world had she just stepped into where Nick was this domestic?

"Not only is it healthier than store bought, but it tastes so much better," he informed her. "No processed chemicals here."

O-kay.

"And do you make other homemade things?" she asked. "Soaps, wreaths or perhaps your suits?"

Now he did laugh as he placed the dough onto

the stone and started arranging it into place. "You're mocking me," he said. "That's fine. I get it. Not many people know that I am actually a great cook."

"So you flip businesses brilliantly, develop high-class resorts and make self-proclaimed famous pizzas." Silvia crossed to the opposite side of the island and settled on a leather stool. "What other secrets are you hiding?"

His eyes darted to hers. A darkness she'd never seen stared back at her, then he glanced back down to his task.

"I'd say that's for another time over something more than pizza."

Silvia watched those strong hands work and couldn't help but recall exactly how talented he had been with her body. As if she needed the reminder. There wasn't a day or night that went by that she didn't remember in vivid detail how perfect they had been together.

And, yes, there had been alcohol involved, but she'd known exactly what she'd been doing and who she'd been saying yes to. Maybe she'd crossed the line because he'd been at a vulnerable time, but he was a big boy. He had definitely been on board with every single passion-filled touch and everything that followed.

Besides, since day one, when he and Lori had come into Silvia's office, there had been sparks. Lingering glances, extra meetings that could probably have been a simple email or text. She'd thought she could work with him and ignore that spark. She'd been wrong.

But she couldn't afford to be wrong again.

"There goes that memory of yours again," he murmured.

Silvia wasn't going to bother denying it this time. Why should she? They both knew this attraction was still strong, and maybe only getting stronger.

"So what if I remember?" she tossed back. "We both had a good time, but that's actually what I'm here to discuss."

With a quirk of a brow, he stilled his hands and stared at her. "Discuss? I prefer no talking, but I'm game to try something new."

Silvia didn't even try to suppress her eye roll. "We have a working relationship, Nick. That's where we need to focus, and that is where this relationship needs to stay."

Nick flattened his hands on the counter and leaned forward. "How long did you rehearse that?"

"Pretty much the entire way over here," she admitted with a smile. "But I'm serious. I have too much at stake to get personally involved with a client."

"Yet you're having my baby, and you still want me."

"Nobody needs to know this is your baby until the project is complete. Actually, I would prefer it that way."

She wasn't going to acknowledge that last part.

If she thought his stare was dark a moment ago, that was nothing compared to what flashed over his face now. Her words had hurt him, angered him. But she had to be honest. It wasn't her way to play games here.

"I will not lie about being the father, and I sure as hell won't stay back and have you go through this process alone."

Silvia completely understood why he was so quick to irritation. He deserved to be part of the baby's life, too.

"That came out wrong," she amended, folding her arms on the concrete countertop. "I'm not pushing you away from our child, but I can't let my firm know that I'm pregnant just yet, and certainly not that I'm pregnant by a client."

Nick stared another minute, his shoulders finally relaxed as he went back to smoothing out the sauce and adding toppings.

"Women don't have babies in your workplace?"

"There are no other women in my workplace."

His eyes darted up to hers. "Seriously? None?"

Silvia shook her head. "There have been in the past, but they've never stayed long. I've just refused to let them drive me out. I'm damn good at my job, I love Green Valley and I need the prestige behind the Baxter firm's name to launch my career."

"You don't need anyone," he replied. "Your prior projects speak volumes about your ability."

While she wished she could bask in the warm fuzzies of his praise, she still had to stay in touch with reality. And the reality was, she worked in a male-dominated field, and more often than not, as a woman, she had to work twice as hard to get half the recognition.

"I'm new to Baxter, remember?" she asked. "I've only been here six months, and I'm still in the probationary period. Besides, I'm sure they wouldn't like to learn that I slept with my very first client. It's important that I be seen as professional."

Nick said nothing as he took the stone and placed it in the brick pizza oven. Now that she glanced around beyond the view, she realized this was a serious chef's kitchen. He had spared no expense with the eight-burner gas stove, two refrigerators and an impressive wine fridge.

Nick circled the island and came to stand next to her, resting his elbow on the counter. His eyes held hers, and she concentrated on keeping his gaze, not letting her focus drop to his lips.

"You are worried about what they'll think, yet that night, you made the first move."

Silvia shrugged. "Sometimes when I see something I want, I go after it. I'm human, and I couldn't stop myself."

He'd had on those glasses with stubble all across his jawline. The combination of rough and studious had been tempting her since they met. But it had been his sense of vulnerability that night that had pushed her over the edge.

Nick inched closer, his hand settling on her thigh. "Something else we have in common. I go after what I want, too."

And then his mouth covered hers.

Five

He was a damn fool for torturing himself.

Nick knew full well that Silvia had every intention of drawing a proverbial line between them of dos and don'ts, but right now all he cared about was feeling her again.

There was no one to stop them, no crew member who could walk in and interrupt. With the pelting rain outside and the aromas wafting around the kitchen, Nick was as relaxed as he had been in weeks. Something about Silvia calmed him…something he couldn't afford to explore further.

His hand slid up her thigh and over her hip to settle at her waist. Silvia shifted in her seat, turning to get a better angle, and her knees widened, so Nick took the opening and settled in deeper.

The softest moan escaped her, and Nick thrust his hand into her hair, tipping her head back just enough to have better access. It still wasn't enough. He wanted to consume her, to strip her of everything and lay her out on the counter. He wanted to carry her out into the rain and take her on the chaise. Anywhere he could have her, he wanted her.

Nick hadn't touched her like this in a month, and no matter what she wanted to claim, their chemistry wasn't just contained to one night. And it wasn't the product of a few too many gin and tonics or the desperation of grief.

There was a passion in Silvia he'd never experienced before, and he wasn't done.

Her hands flattened against his chest, and she pushed him slightly. "No. We can't do this."

Actually, they could, because they were, but he respected her enough to stop. She was obviously torn, and he didn't want to make her life more difficult.

"Why would you deny yourself?" he asked.

"Because I have a job to do, and now I have a child to consider," she stated. "Right now, my needs are irrelevant."

At least she admitted she had needs. That was a step in the right direction. He was just going to help her take another step. She felt this heat between them just as he did, and she could only deny herself for so long...

"Obligations are something I understand," he stated. "I wouldn't be where I am today if I hadn't always held firm to my responsibilities. But it's okay to be selfish sometimes."

Her eyes darted away. "I have been selfish my entire life," she murmured.

"I find that difficult to believe."

Nick doubted there was a selfish bone in her body. When someone worked as hard as she did, was as determined as she was, that meant often putting other people's needs first.

"You don't know me, Nick." Her eyes flashed back to his, pain and sorrow settling deep in them. "My childhood wasn't quite as sweet as yours."

Nick eased back from between her legs and settled on a bar stool. He reached across the island and slid his hand over hers. Those words weren't what he was expecting, and he realized he didn't know enough about her. He actually wanted to know more.

More than what it felt like to be with her for one night, more than how much ass she could kick as an architect. Nick wasn't sure what that meant—that he wanted to know everything about her—but he wasn't going to try to label his emotions, not when they were all so raw.

"I grew up pretty damn poor," he told her when she remained silent. "I didn't know just how poor at the time. My mother never let me feel like I was un-loved or that we weren't safe."

"Well, I never knew my parents."

A sad smile crept over her face, and it took every ounce of willpower not to haul her into his lap. Nick waited for her to continue, but the pit in his stom-ach told him he wasn't going to like what she had to say. This shocking revelation was a far cry from the lifestyle he'd assumed she'd had while growing up. Maybe they were more alike than he thought, both having difficult pasts to overcome before find-ing success.

"I was sent to my first foster home two days after I was born."

Her voice remained strong, as if she'd become numb to the past, or as if she'd given this rundown too many times to be affected and now they were just words. But Nick knew better. Silvia felt deeply; she was invested in this story about how she'd been raised. She'd put up a defensive wall against her past, and that was how she was able to talk about it now. As if he needed another reason to admire her. The more he discovered about her, the more he was piec-ing together how she'd become so strong and resilient.

"By the time I started school, I had been in three foster homes. From then on, I continued to bounce around. There were times I caused trouble, and I re-member a counselor telling the couple I was living with that I just needed more attention."

Silvia's humorless laugh pierced his heart. There was so much pain in the sound, he wondered if she even realized how much.

"Attention was the last thing I wanted," she went on. "I wanted to be left alone. I excelled at school because that's what I threw myself into. The only thing I connected with was reading, so I read everything I got my hands on."

"My mother used to read to me every night," he chimed in, unusually comfortable with talking about his own past. "Even when I was a teenager, that was something I never got tired of. I knew it was something not everyone did, so I never told a soul, but it was our thing."

Silvia offered him a sweet smile. "A little library for the baby is a good idea. I don't think it's ever too early to start showing them how much you care."

From a woman who clearly wanted someone to care. Maybe that's exactly what she'd always needed. She might put up that steely exterior, but hurt recognized hurt. No matter how much she kept to herself, Silvia deserved someone in her life she could count on…someone she could turn to.

That certainly wasn't him. He wasn't the type of man who had ever longed for family life. He'd watched his mother work hard to save every penny, and she'd taught him how to have a strong work ethic so he could have a better life than anything she could've provided in his early years. She'd instilled in him that his career had to come first because he couldn't always count on a relationship to put food on the table, or for happiness.

Growing up without a father had been a void he never could shake, and now that he knew the truth, that void seemed to be even larger because of who his father really was. There was so much ugliness surrounding Rusty Lockwood, and that bloodline lived in Nick. Maybe that bloodline was more a part of him than he could have imagined. Was Rusty's legacy why he'd failed at his first marriage? Was it why he couldn't see himself as father material? Maybe it confirmed that he wasn't a man worthy to be with Silvia.

Even so, he would provide for her and their child.

Nick didn't like the poignant stirrings swirling like a vortex inside his heart. He couldn't let his emotions get wrapped up in her right now, especially with the state he was in. Now was certainly not the time to make any major life decisions or read too much into what was happening between them. All he could offer her was a physical connection and financial support—he had plenty of both to give.

The timer went off before he could say anything else. Nick stood, and Silvia came to her feet as well.

"I should go."

Nick settled his hands on her shoulders and looked her in the eyes. "Dinner is ready, and it's getting nasty out. Stay."

Her eyes held his, and he waited for her to argue or decline, but she simply nodded.

"I'd like that."

"We're still within budget and on track to open by summer's end," Silvia stated as she leaned back in the Adirondack chair on the covered patio.

Dinner had been amazing, and Nick deserved those bragging rights he'd talked about earlier. Somehow, he'd convinced her to come outside to watch the storm, and she found the longer she sat here, the more relaxed and comfortable she became. So she opted to discuss work and try to keep her mind centered right where it should be.

"That's good news," Nick told her. "I'm sure something will come up with the budget—that's inevitable with older buildings—but I want this done right and exactly how my mom would've envisioned it. I'm not worried about the cost."

No, he wouldn't be. Not only did he have the financial means to do anything he wanted, he would spare no expense in honoring the woman he'd loved more than anyone.

That kind of bond was a true testament to the type of man Nick was. She believed he would be loyal to a fault, but Silvia also didn't know how all of this would work between them and with the baby.

Regardless, she had several months to get a sense of his true feelings about being a father. No matter what, she would provide for their child, whether Nick decided to be in the picture or not.

"Have you been able to lock in that licensing you wanted for the bar?" she asked, keeping the conversation on business…a safer common ground.

Nick let out a snort. "Not yet. Rusty Lockwood is a bastard on his best day, but I'm not done with him. The fight won't end until I've won."

"I haven't met him, but I've been in town long enough to know he has more enemies than friends. The tourists don't seem to mind, though. His establishment is always busy."

"Tourists are there for the tasting experience and the liquor to take home," Nick stated. "They don't care about the type of man Rusty is. And his so-called friends are paid to remain loyal, so I'm not sure how legit those relationships are."

Yeah, she'd heard all about how much of a shark Rusty was. His moonshine distillery brought in thousands of thirsty tourists per month and was good for the local economy, but the man only cared about the bottom line. He'd been under a lot of scrutiny recently, from what Silvia had heard. Only last year he had been fined by the IRS for tax evasion.

Maybe he'd made some enemies way back when he'd first started and moonshine was illegal. Rusty couldn't pay off everybody who passed through that he needed on his side. Silvia was just glad she didn't have to deal with the infamous mogul.

"I'm sure you'll win the fight," she told Nick. "You have more motivation to win than he does."

"I've never lost a fight yet," he informed her. "I sure as hell don't intend to lose this time, not to such an arrogant prick."

Silvia extended her legs out in front of her and crossed her ankles. Lacing her hands over her abdomen, she closed her eyes as she listened to the rain and the roll of thunder. She wondered about the little life growing inside her and could admit she was equal parts terrified and excited.

Even though she'd never really had a solid mother figure, Silvia vowed to do her absolute best where this baby was concerned. Love and stability would go a long way.

Nick's arm brushed hers, and she wished when they'd come out that he'd chosen another seat—he had enough choices, between the benches, loungers, and tables and chairs, but he'd taken up in the Adirondack next to hers.

The nearness did nothing to tamp down her desires. Having him cook dinner for her hadn't helped, either. Getting even more involved with him would not look good to her firm—it was the reason she'd never intended to be intimate with him again—and part of her wondered if they were waiting on her to mess up just like this. Not that they'd ever admit it, because they thrived on having a solid reputation, but she figured Clark was ready to swoop in and take over the project at her first slip.

Fingertips brushed over her arm, then feathered across her cheek.

"Silvia."

Her name sounded so distant, yet so intimate.

"Sil."

Nobody ever called her that. Having her one-time lover use a special name should have made her want to run away for fear of getting entangled in something she wasn't ready for. But she couldn't run from Nick, not anymore…and she didn't want to.

His fingertips slid over her jawline, and a moment later she was being lifted, cradled.

Her eyes flew open as she realized Nick had swept her up into his arms. "What are you doing?"

"You fell asleep."

With a strength she found ridiculously sexy, he carried her through the house. She slid her arms around his neck for a more secure hold. Maybe just for a minute she'd allow herself to take comfort in his warmth and strength.

"I can walk, you know."

"I'm aware. You actually have quite a sexy strut."

Silvia narrowed her eyes. "I don't strut."

"Oh, you do."

He turned toward the grand staircase and started up. "What are you doing?"

The stubborn man wasn't even out of breath as

he hit the first landing and kept going on up to the second floor.

"Putting you to bed."

"Oh, hell no."

Nick's deep chuckle vibrated against her. "Relax. I have plenty of spare bedrooms. You can even choose which one you want. They all have their own baths and their own views of the mountains."

"I'm not worried about the amenities," she countered. "I can't spend the night."

When he reached the top, he stopped and glanced down at her. "You said the same about dinner, but you enjoyed it. Two of everything, if I recall."

"I do everything in twos," she muttered, hating that he had noticed that little quirk.

Silvia growled when he remained still and staring. "Put me down."

The arm beneath her knees gave way, and she gripped his neck to keep from stumbling as she found her footing.

"I'm not staying," she repeated.

Nick settled his hands on the curve of her hips and leveled a stare. "I don't recall you being so difficult when we first started working together. In fact, we got along so well."

Yeah, hence the pregnancy. They'd had that whole flirtatious-banter thing going on for months before she decided to make a move.

After all the pep talks she'd given herself on why

she couldn't get involved with a client, she'd had a moment of weakness and given in to her desires. Denying Nick wasn't something she could do, and she'd honestly thought one night would simply be just that…one night only. They'd agreed not to discuss it again.

And they hadn't. Until she'd found out she was pregnant. Keeping a personal distance at that point had become utterly impossible.

"Everything has changed," she reminded him. "I work for you. I can't play roommates or have a slumber party with you, too."

His mouth twitched, and she wanted to smack him. "I'm serious," she added.

"Nobody has to know you're here," he told her. "Nobody has to know you're pregnant or that I'm the father until you're ready. I respect the position you're in, and I'm sure we're both going to learn along the way. Don't push me away just because you're scared."

Scared? She had well surpassed scared. There was no plan B if she lost her job. She'd had to depend on herself nearly her entire life, and now was no different. Wait, it was totally different, because now she would have a little human who depended on her for financial stability and loving support.

And Nick wanted her to stay, agreeing to carry over the terms from their one-night stand, not letting anyone in on their secrets.

A good portion of her was tempted to take him up on his offer. They'd been so compatible in bed, and she never ignored warning flags and did something for herself.

But, as tempted as she was, she also had to keep her control in place. One little slip and she'd find herself in Nick's bed before she could even see that red flag waving.

Silvia stared back at him and then shook her head. "I can't figure you out. You say the right things, you do the right things, you're…"

Apparently her exhaustion and attraction had removed the filter from her mouth.

"Don't stop now," Nick said with a sexy grin. "I'm interested in knowing what you think about me."

"Your ego is big enough," she chided. "I'm not feeding it any more than necessary."

Nick smoothed her hair away from her face, and Silvia pulled up all of her control to ignore the urge to turn her face into his touch.

"It's not my ego that needs feeding." His eyes held hers for a second before he shifted that hungry focus to her lips. "I have other urges." He nipped at her lips. "Other desires."

The dim lights lining the hall set an intimate mood she couldn't afford. The late hour, the storm surging outside, the way he looked at her like he was ready to fulfill her every need, the way she wanted him in spite of her best intentions, all collided into a dangerous situation.

"This is a terrible idea," she whispered, but she found herself reaching up to touch his crisp stubble that would no doubt turn back into the beard he typically sported. "I came here to tell you we couldn't be more than professional colleagues for now and we would work on the whole parenting thing later."

Nick gripped her hips and pulled her closer. "You did tell me, several times, in fact."

"I'm not taking my own advice."

Nick eased closer until his lips were a breath away. "Nobody knows you're here, Silvia. Nobody has to know what we do behind closed doors. And this attraction has nothing to do with business."

Why did his every word resonate with her? Why did she want to ignore everything outside this house and just take what he offered?

Because she was human and she wanted him and resisting Nick had proven to be impossible...not that she tried too hard, but still.

Before common sense could prevail, Silvia framed his face with her hands and covered her mouth with his. Once again, he swept her up into his arms, and this time, she didn't object.

Six

Nick fully expected Silvia to argue or insist on leaving. He'd been ready to accept he might have to let her go, even though taking her into his suite was exactly where he'd wanted her since day one.

Now she was here, and she looked even more perfect than he'd imagined.

Lightning flashed through the wall of windows and doors in his bedroom. He wanted to see her in this light. In the frantic, raging storm. The fury seemed fitting, considering they both were going into this knowing they might be making a mistake, arguing about the reasons they should be more careful, but ultimately agreeing they deserved to take what they wanted.

For two people who had been in the deepest valleys of life as children, they knew that when happiness entered the realm, they had to take hold.

"Tell me now if you don't want this."

Her eyes held his as she reached down and pulled her silky top over her head and tossed it to the floor.

"Just one more night," she told him. "Tomorrow we go back to being architect and client."

Sure, if she wanted to tell herself that, he could play the game. And maybe she even believed the lies she told herself, but there was still too much heat between them. Ultimately there was no way they could keep up the professional charade she was hoping for.

"You're feeling all right?" he asked. "I mean, with the baby?"

"The baby and I are both fine," she assured him. "I wouldn't keep anything like that from you."

Her affirmation of loyalty shouldn't tug at his...

No. His heart wasn't involved.

That was absurd. This was lust and sex. They had limits on their crazy attraction. Neither of them wanted more, and he should be ecstatic she felt the same.

Nick was done talking, because talking only revealed more and more ways they were alike and compatible. He quickly rid himself of his clothes, but when Silvia started to reach for her pants, he swiped her hands away.

"I'll do this."

With expert work on the button and zipper, he

had her jeans sliding down shapely thighs, leaving her standing in her satin panties and matching bra.

Nick slid his hands over her curves, grazing his thumbs over her abdomen. He dropped to his knees and kissed the smooth skin just below her belly button.

Silvia's fingers threaded through his hair, and instead of getting wrapped up in the turmoil of his life lately, Nick dipped his head to the curve of her inner thigh and trailed kisses along the delicate elastic seam where her panties met skin. He gripped her hips and inhaled her arousal, his body throbbing with a need he only found with her.

And this time they were both completely sober.

He curled his fingers around the material and pulled her panties down until she lifted one foot then the other to kick them aside.

Nick gripped the back of one leg and lifted it over his shoulder as he buried his face at her core. Silvia's cry and the tug on his hair had Nick grabbing hold of her backside to secure her exactly where they both wanted. He'd had every intention of going slow and properly laying her on his bed like a gentleman.

But when it came to his desires, there wasn't a gentlemanly thought on his mind. Something inside him snapped whenever she moaned or sighed or gave any inclination that every move he was making was the right one. He got so much intense pleasure from *her* pleasure that Nick could continue for hours.

Silvia's hips jerked, and she cried out his name

as her orgasm tore through her. Nick consumed her release, making sure she had the best experience, because this was just the beginning of the night. He wanted so much more from this passionate woman.

When her trembling ceased, Nick held on to her as he came to his feet. She swayed a little against him, and he swept her back up into his arms.

Before tonight, he hadn't realized how much he loved doing this, but holding Silvia in such a protective pose made him feel like he could shield her from anything life threw her way. She deserved that, even though she'd argue she didn't need anybody.

"You're determined to carry me everywhere," she murmured, laying her head against his shoulder.

"Oh, I'm determined," he agreed, but his motivation was a little more primal.

Now he did lay her out on the bed, selfishly standing over her to take in that flushed body. With the exterior lights and the random flashes of lightning, he could see her perfectly.

Silvia came up onto her elbows and smiled. "Are you joining me, or do you think I'm going to beg?"

Nick laughed as he climbed up on the bed to settle over her. She fell back and wrapped her arms and legs around him.

"Protection?" he asked, realizing that might be silly at this point, but there were other issues besides an unplanned pregnancy.

"I'm clean," she told him. "You?"

He nodded. "Is this what you want?"

Because going without would put them at an entirely different level of intimacy—one he wasn't sure either of them was ready for.

Yet he couldn't deny his wants or her obvious desire.

Nick joined their bodies and earned a gasp from Silvia as she arched against him. He gritted his teeth as he began to move, confirming that the one night he'd had with her *had* been different...euphoric.

With one hand on the back of her thigh and the other holding his body above hers, Nick shifted against her as she met his thrusts with her own. Her passion matched his, and Nick still couldn't get enough.

Watching Silvia with her head tossed back, biting on her bottom lip, with a sheen of perspiration dotting her chest and neck, was just about the sexiest thing he'd ever seen.

Her hands came up to grip his shoulders, her short nails bit into his skin. She panted his name as her expressive eyes focused onto his, and then she utterly came apart once again. Nick could only appreciate the erotic sight for a moment before his own climax slammed into him.

Nick closed his eyes, afraid of looking at her for fear of what she'd see. He was too raw, too vulnerable right now, but he'd never admit such things. They'd agreed this was just sex, and that's all he was taking from her...all he was willing to give.

"That's two," he murmured against her ear when their bodies calmed and he settled in beside her.

With a soft chuckle, Silvia nestled against him, and it was no time before her breathing slowed. He was left awake, alone with his thoughts about how to tackle his past and not ruin his future.

Nick pulled into Hawkins Bourbon Distillery to meet up with owner Sam Hawkins. This newer distillery had been around for a decade, but that was young in the industry, especially considering how long bourbon needed to age. But Sam's gin, rye and vodka had exploded onto the scene.

Since he couldn't sell in Green Valley, Hawkins was huge in larger cities across the country and trickling into the overseas market.

Now Hawkins was gearing up to launch their first ten-year bourbon while thousands of others continued to age in the barrels.

Sam had made quite a name for himself in Green Valley, and nationally, for the spirits he pushed out. Nick knew it was true because tours of this place sold out months in advance. This little gold mine produced some of the best gin that Nick had ever tasted, and he wanted it for his resort. He'd had a few samplings that first night with Silvia, but that wasn't something he could dwell on now. Today was all about seeing how he and Sam could make this partnership happen when Rusty was determined to stand in their way.

So Nick was going straight to the top to see if he and Sam could work together in teaming up against Rusty and his band of crooked city cronies. Nick didn't know Sam on a personal level, but Nick had toured the distillery before and was more than impressed with the company.

Nick made his way up the stony path that led to the main building. Sam had made sure to keep the old charm of the brick and stone buildings while adding an updated feel with the thick, square columns leading up to the second-story tasting deck, and he'd added a glassed-in area overlooking the lake in the back. Nick recalled from the tour he had taken before that the offset room was for special parties or elite groups.

The gas lamps on each of the posts and on either side of the fifteen-foot double doors were a perfect nod to the history of the place. Nick appreciated all of the details and wouldn't mind taking some of these ideas back to his own resort.

Sam was expecting him, so Nick bypassed the lines of people waiting to check in for various tours and headed down a long hallway that ultimately ended at the base of a winding staircase. Nick climbed the steps, and at the top was a young man at a desk, who greeted him with a smile.

"You must be Nick Campbell. Sam is expecting you."

The guy gestured to another hallway, and Nick nodded his thanks and headed down. The old wood floors and iron sconces on the gray walls kept that same masculine vibe and old-world theme as the rest of the place. The Hawkins emblem had been embedded into the wood floors.

Nick reached the door and tapped his knuckles on the frame.

"Come in," a voice stated from the other side.

Nick eased open the door and was surprised at the vast office with an entire wall of glass overlooking the creek running behind the distillery. All distilleries had to be near fresh water, rich with limestone. That was just another thing that made Green Valley so perfect for these types of businesses—plenty of fresh water sources.

"Nick Campbell."

Sam Hawkins rose from his desk and came around with his arm extended. Nick crossed to shake his hand and was shocked by the sheer size of the guy. He'd seen pictures, but nothing prepared him for the Jason Momoa look-alike.

"Thanks for seeing me," Nick said as he released the strong grip and adjusted the frames of his glasses. "I won't take up too much of your time."

Sam crossed his arms over his chest and leaned

back onto his desk. "Take all the time you need. I'm always eager to discuss bourbon."

The CEO might look large and menacing, but he seemed genuine and certainly didn't have the stuffy appearance and attitude of a stereotypical chief executive. He wore a Hawkins Bourbon tee and jeans, a very non-CEO wardrobe that Nick could easily relate to. Gone were the days of business owners always wearing suits and ties.

"I'll get to the point," Nick stated. "I'm opening a new mountain resort in late August. I want Hawkins to be the exclusive gin and bourbon."

Sam stared for a minute before he laughed. "I'd love to, but you know that's not going to happen with Rusty Lockwood controlling the damn licenses. He'll only approve it if you exclusively use his hard liquor."

"That's why I'm here in person," Nick went on, knowing anything worth having was worth working for. "I think with two powerhouses teaming up, he won't want to take on both of us. Especially if we can show numbers to the city council and provide statistics on how much growth our businesses can and will bring to Green Valley. Money speaks louder than Rusty Lockwood."

Sam seemed to mull over that nugget of information. Nick wasn't about to mention that Rusty was his biological father. That loaded fact would be the perfect blackmail for Rusty should he choose to fight back.

Nick didn't want to lay that card out just yet with anyone...including Rusty.

"That bastard has been a pain in my ass for years," Sam finally said. "He's offered to buy me out countless times, but I'll die first before I let him get his hands on my company."

Nick knew from that statement alone that Sam would be all for this partnership. Just another step forward in gaining everything Nick needed to fulfill his mother's dream.

"He sees me as a threat," Sam went on. "If he could push his ego aside and understand moonshine and bourbon draw totally different crowds, maybe he'd think differently. Some people like both, but most people prefer one or the other. But he's stubborn, and he's mean. Any business dealings with him are off the table for me. No merging, no partnering, no selling."

Sounded like they were both on the same page in their hatred for the moonshine mogul. Rusty was seriously only hurting himself by trying to monopolize this region.

If Rusty continued to commit career suicide, it was only a matter of time before Nick could come in and take over. Who knows, maybe he'd buy out Lockwood Lightning one day down the road. Wouldn't that be poetic justice?

"I'm popping into a poker game tomorrow night," Nick told Sam. "Rusty plays every weekend with some city council members, and I found out where their boys' club location is. The Rogue Wingman's back room."

Sam nodded and raised his brows. "I'm impressed. You really want this."

A flash of his mother's elegant handwriting on the letter whipped through his mind. "More than anything."

Sam pushed away from the desk and gestured toward the door. "Let's go have a drink and discuss the details. If you're ready to take on Lockwood, I sure as hell am not going to miss that chance. And I agree. With both of us coming at him, he might change his tune."

Nick wasn't going to turn down the drink or the discussion about how they could work together. Maybe this alliance would turn into something even more powerful than either of them expected.

Seven

"Delivery for you."

Silvia glanced up from the design she had been perfecting for the main check-in desk at Nick's resort. She couldn't quite get the layout to present the way she wanted it. Something was off, and she had been staring and staring but still couldn't put her finger on it.

When she spotted the office receptionist, she did a double take at the desk chair with a giant red bow wrapped around it in her doorway.

"Delivery?" she asked, coming to her feet. "A chair?"

"That's what I was told by the guy who dropped it off."

Silvia rounded her desk and glanced at the oversize leather piece. There was an envelope with her name on it dangling from the bow.

She glanced to the receptionist. "Thanks, Kevin. I'll take it from here."

Once he was gone, Silvia wheeled the chair in and closed her door. Most people received flowers or chocolate or a tacky dancing bear or something. But…furniture?

She tore open the envelope and read the card.

"I researched and these were the best chairs for expecting moms."

No signature, but she knew who this was from, and her moment of surprise quickly turned into anger. He couldn't just have a chair delivered here. She was perfectly fine in her old chair. And what if Kevin had gotten nosy and opened the envelope? Considering it was still sealed when she got to it, she knew he hadn't, but he *could have*.

Silvia pushed the chair into the corner and went back to her perfectly fine seat. She tucked the note into her purse to make sure no other eyes saw the message before she pulled out her phone and completely bypassed a text message. This situation warranted a phone call.

"Silvia. I was just thinking about you."

Nick's answer had her gripping her cell and turning to look out the window. "I bet, considering you just had one of your minions make a delivery to my office and then slink out before I caught him."

His low laughter sent a shiver through her. She didn't want those shivers—she wanted to be angry.

"Minion?" Nick asked still laughing. "I'll be sure to let Garret know his new title."

"Listen," she said in a lower tone. "You can't have things delivered here…or anywhere else, for that matter. And you most definitely need to watch what you write and what you say."

The laughter on the other end died, and Nick cleared his throat. "I didn't even think about that," he stated. "I was up doing some research last night and I wanted you to have the best, because I know how important your work is to you."

Well, damn it. Not only did he recognize her career and its value to her, but he also took the time to see what would be best for her and the baby. Her anger vanished, quickly replaced by a warmth she didn't have room for in her life. She *wanted* to be angry. It was easier. She wanted that sliver of negativity so she could justify pushing Nick away…but he continued to turn everything to the good.

"I can take it back if you don't want it," he added.

Silvia stared at the leather chair with padded arms and a curved back and shook her head. "No. I'm being a jerk when I should have just called to say thank you instead of berating you."

"You're welcome. I'll be more careful, but I won't stop taking care of what's mine."

Silvia opened her mouth, but before she could say a word, Nick went on.

"I'm well aware that you can take care of yourself, but you're carrying my child."

With a whirl of emotions spiraling through her, Silvia crossed her office and sank into the new chair. The leather seemed to hug her body, and she couldn't deny that she was already in love with this darn thing…and she hadn't even hit any buttons to take advantage of all the features.

"I need to go," he told her. "And don't be angry about the next shipment."

The next…

What?

Silvia glanced to the phone and saw he'd disconnected the call. What the hell did he mean by *the next shipment*? She had specifically told him not to do anything else…which clearly meant he had another plan already in play.

Great, now she would be on edge all day waiting for who knew what to show up at her office door. Maybe it would be something as simple as flowers. He couldn't keep sending furniture…could he?

But flowers seemed normal and romantic and not quite right for them. They weren't actually dating or trying to forge a normal relationship. Nothing about this arrangement was normal—but she wouldn't turn down some fresh blooms.

Pushing aside the silly daydream, Silvia wheeled

away her old chair and put her new one in place. She'd have to have someone come get this old one, but she wasn't quite ready to answer questions, so she tucked it into the corner for now.

As she stared down at the design she'd been working on moments ago, she couldn't help but wonder what else Nick had up his sleeve…and why she found his tendency to surprise her so damn attractive.

Silvia pulled into her drive and stared at the boxes on her front porch. She hadn't ordered anything, so she had to assume this was Nick's second installment for the day. What on earth had he done now?

At least this present had come to her home and not her office. She'd had to dodge some questioning gazes earlier when she'd had her old desk chair removed. She'd played it off that she just wanted something cozier and she'd had it delivered to herself…bow and all.

Lame, but she couldn't think of anything else.

She pulled her car into the garage and grabbed her purse before heading out and around to the stone sidewalk. She followed the curved path to her porch and recognized the label on the boxes as that from her favorite local restaurant, Mama Jane's.

He'd had food delivered? She certainly wasn't turning that down, and if any of these three boxes had her favorite banana cream pie, she might just propose to Nick Campbell.

Silvia laughed at herself as she unlocked the front door and took her boxes inside, one at a time. Marriage was ridiculous. They'd had amazing sex, they were having a baby, but the food delivery was what drove her to think marriage? Clearly, she had problems.

There was no note with the boxes, but Silvia knew. Other than her coworkers, she really hadn't had time to make friends or go out and socialize since coming to town. Nick was the one constant in her life, both professional and personal.

Silvia took each box into her kitchen and opened them to see what Nick had sent.

As she pulled out the packing that had kept the food cold and fresh so she could cook it when she wanted, she realized there was two of everything… including the banana cream pie. He'd remembered.

The familiar burn hit her throat a moment before her eyes filled. Crazy pregnancy hormones. Who knew cartons of pot pies, biscuits and desserts would set her off?

She put each package into her refrigerator and set the larger packing boxes out of the way. She'd never had anyone go to the trouble of taking care of her before. Part of her balked at the idea of not being solely independent—she'd been on her own for so long—but the other part of her realized Nick wasn't trying to steal her identity. He was trying to help her and feel like he was needed.

There would be some push/pull as they figured out all of this, but Silvia had to remain true to herself and do what was best for the baby. Contemplating a relationship just because she had warm and fuzzy feelings was a complete mistake.

Silvia had once mistaken lust for something more. After coming out of a multitude of foster homes, she'd turned eighteen and set off on her own with her boyfriend of two months. After a quick courthouse wedding and a month of not-so-wedded bliss, she'd realized her mistake.

Since then, Silvia had shied away from anything akin to a relationship. How would she know what was right? She couldn't trust her own judgment, her own emotions, because she had never been shown the right way.

Despite her upbringing, Silvia knew one thing for certain. She would love this baby and always provide a shelter and a safe haven, because no child should ever have to wonder if they were loved or secure.

Just as she reached for her purse to grab her cell, the phone rang. Smiling, she glanced to the screen, fully expecting to see Nick's name. That wasn't the case.

"John, what's up?"

"We have a problem," the foreman from Nick's resort responded. "I tried calling Mr. Campbell, but he didn't answer. There was an accident, and we have an injured worker. The ambulance is here now."

Silvia immediately grabbed her purse and headed

out the back door toward her garage. "I'm on my way. I'll try getting in touch with Nick."

She disconnected the call and prayed the entire way to the site that the worker would be okay and there would be no backlash on her or the firm or Nick.

On-site accidents weren't uncommon, but there were too many variables, and Silvia sure as hell hoped none of this was due to negligence on her end. She could not afford to screw up on her first project, especially not one of this magnitude.

She had so many questions that wouldn't and couldn't be answered until she got to the site. She wondered why they were there so late on a Friday. It was well after six o'clock, and they typically were done by five.

As Silvia made her way to the resort, she tried calling Nick but only got his voice mail. Where was he? The man always had his phone. She'd never had an issue with getting in touch with him about the project before.

Silvia could handle this, but Nick needed to be there—he needed to know what was going on. After two voice mails and an SOS text, she pulled into the site and rushed to the scene to see exactly what she was dealing with.

Rusty Lockwood's tired, deep-set eyes widened as Nick stepped into the closed poker room. That shocked gaze shifted over Nick's shoulder to Sam, and the old bastard nearly dropped his cards.

Oh, the element of surprise was already working in their favor.

"Got room for two more?" Nick asked, not waiting for an answer as he settled in at the round felt table.

The room reeked of cigar smoke and moonshine. The suits of the town had shed their jackets and ties, and their sleeves were all rolled up. Nick recognized several men—some he had already butted heads with over the liquor license.

Sam took a seat next to him, and they both pulled out their wallets, flashing their Benjamins. Rusty's stare volleyed between Nick and Sam, and it took everything in Nick not to stare in return, looking to find any physical similarities. He'd wondered his entire life about his father, and now he sat in the same room with him but couldn't say a word.

Not that he wanted to. Nick wasn't happy about the paternity facts, and he sure as hell wasn't looking for some loving reunion. Just because Rusty was Nick's father didn't mean Nick needed that bond. That was something in his life he'd never have, but he would be damn sure his child never knew this kind of void.

Nick's sole purpose tonight was to make sure Rusty knew who he was up against and to face the very real reality that Nick wasn't backing down. Ever. Not only was he not backing down, he was building an army to rise up against Rusty. The days of Rusty Lockwood running Green Valley and the surrounding counties were coming to an end.

Nick didn't want to take his business—that had never been the issue. Nick just wanted the old mogul to do the right thing—to open up Green Valley to new blood and to stop being such a dick. Apparently all of that was too much to ask.

Whatever. Nick wasn't intimidated in the slightest and Sam was just another ace in the hole. Nick and Sam had a mutual hatred for the moonshine kingpin.

"Get you fellas a drink?" an older man asked as he came to his feet and headed to the bar in the corner. He held up a familiar tall, rectangular bottle with a dome-shaped lid. A lightning bolt down the front was a sign everyone easily recognized.

Sam shook his head as he fanned out his cards. "Not much of a moonshine fan."

Nick bit the inside of his cheek to keep from laughing. "I'll take a bourbon."

"Just the white lightning served here," the old guy stated, putting the bottle back on the counter. "Never seen anyone turn down perfectly good moonshine."

"Show me good moonshine and I won't turn it down," Nick joked, which earned a few chuckles, but not from Russ. "Five-card stud? My favorite. Deal us in."

Nick's cell vibrated in his pocket, but he ignored it. On a Friday night, he had nothing else he needed to be doing other than this right here. Besides his unborn child, all that mattered was pushing through to fulfill his mother's wishes and their ultimate goal. Nick planned on fighting this battle not just for his business, but for Sam and for other establishments like theirs.

Over the next half hour, he won a couple hands, Sam won a hand and Rusty grew angrier by the minute. Even his tumbler of moonshine had gone untouched, and his cigar had sat in the tray completely ignored. He must be really pissed…which only pleased Nick further. Good. The man needed to learn that not everything would go his way in life.

The cell in his pocket had vibrated off and on for the past hour, but Nick played on. He'd catch up when he left. He'd waited too long to make his next move and he couldn't let anything interrupt.

"You're the one working on that resort over on Silversmith Mountain, right?"

Nick glanced to the older gentleman who'd initially offered him a drink. "That's me. Should be open at the end of summer."

"This town can always use more places like that, at the rate people flock here."

Nick fully agreed as he motioned for another card. "I'm banking on just that. But my mother had a bigger vision, so we're doing a few extras that other getaways don't have."

"He's about to open a gold mine," Sam stated as

he folded and eased back in his seat. "The economy is great around here. More resorts and places to stay means more people coming to the distillery."

Rusty grunted as he folded his hand. He reached for his glass and swirled it around. It was moonshine, not an aged bourbon or an expensive wine. The man seriously needed a lesson in fine alcohol.

Nick rested his hand on the green felt and waited for the other players to reveal their cards. Nick kept his poker face in place as he laid down aces over jacks and raked in the winnings.

"You play often?" another man asked.

"Not as often as I'd like," Nick replied with a grin.

"I doubt I can afford to play with you every week," Sam joked. "But I'll let you take my money tonight."

Nick stacked his chips and weighed his next words carefully as he glanced to Sam.

"Oh, you'll get plenty of my money once we're in business together."

Sam simply nodded without glancing up as he reached for the new cards he'd been dealt. Nick left the veiled statement hanging and didn't even glance up to Rusty. He didn't need to see the old man's reaction to know he'd hit home, and looking across the table would only be seen as a direct threat. Nick figured he and Sam showing up together and that carefully laid-out business venture was warning enough for one night.

After about an hour, and multiple wins, Nick came

to his feet. "Well, guys, I'll head on out, but I'll be back next week, if you're taking new members."

Every man in the room, save for Nick and Sam, glanced to Rusty, who looked like he was about to explode—if the red face and flared nostrils were any indicators. He better get used to being pissed off because Nick was going to really upset his perfect little world.

"We're not taking new members," Rusty finally answered, glaring at Nick from across the table. "I don't know how you managed to get in here tonight, but it was a onetime thing."

And he wouldn't find out how Nick and Sam managed to get in. Rusty wasn't the only one with power in this town.

Nick started to ease forward, but Sam put a hand on his shoulder.

"We'll see," Sam stated. "Seems your friends didn't mind the extras."

After a good ten-second stare, Nick pulled back from the table and gave a nod to the other men. Then he followed Sam out of the smoke-filled room and pulled in fresh air once they were out of the back of the restaurant.

"Well, that went well." Sam laughed. "It was tempting to see what you were going to do, but I wanted to get us both out of there in good standing— and I don't have time for jail."

Nick shook his head and flexed his hands at his

sides. "I wouldn't have hit him. I've been tempted for years, but I won't let him get the best of me or give him the satisfaction."

They headed down the narrow brick street toward the parking lot.

"So I'll meet you here next week? Same time?" Sam asked.

Nick nodded. "Counting on it."

Sam turned toward where he'd parked, jumped in his car and headed out. Nick turned the opposite way to head to his truck as he pulled his cell from his pocket and saw all the missed calls and texts.

It didn't take long for him to realize he'd missed a hell of a problem while trying to deal with another.

Nick made record time getting to the site and only hoped Silvia was okay and the injured worker wouldn't sue.

Of all the times for him to have gone silent, this was quite possibly the worst. He cursed himself the entire way to Silversmith Mountain. His first thought when he'd seen her name so many times on his screen was that something had happened to her or the baby.

He didn't want to acknowledge what that sickening pit in his stomach told him. He cared about Silvia so much more than he should've ever allowed.

Now what the hell was he going to do about that complication?

Eight

"Well, I'm glad you could make it."

Silvia stood over the broken, splintered floor where the worker had fallen and thankfully only suffered a twisted ankle and some scratches to his arms.

For the past hour and a half, she'd been trying to get in touch with Nick, but he'd obviously been too busy to answer his phone or worry about his business. The longer she surveyed the area and the more she talked to the foreman, the angrier she became. The accident stemmed from a worker who had stayed late on his own to finish some work. Supposedly when he was sanding the flooring, he had mishandled the equipment, resulting in the brittle planks giving way.

Silvia wasn't so sure she knew what to believe,

because the inspector had been out multiple times and found the floors were solid.

Since everyone had left, she'd tried to wrap her mind around the events of the evening, but she was tired and wanted to just go home. This was certainly one drawback of the job she so loved.

She wished Nick had arrived more quickly, wished he would take more care in his responsibilities to this resort, because they had to work as a team…especially now.

Maybe he'd been on a date. The thought slammed into her and caused her pause. They hadn't discussed whether or not they'd see other people and it's not like they were in a committed relationship with each other…right?

She didn't like the weight of jealousy that settled deep within her.

"I came as soon as I could," he told her, carefully stepping over the construction zone. "Fill me in."

Silvia glanced over her shoulder, surprised he already had on his hard hat. "One of the workers was negligent, and he now has a twisted ankle. That's the gist. The long story is that you weren't available when the foreman called or when I called and texted. I'm not sure who she was, but if you could tell your dates that you have other obligations—"

Nick took hold of her shoulders. "Dates? You think I was on a date? If I wasn't pissed at the accusation, I'd think you were jealous."

Jealous? Please. She wasn't jealous.

She *wasn't*. Being jealous would imply that they had a committed relationship to each other—which they didn't.

"From a professional angle, I deserve to have my calls answered," she retorted. "This is your property, and you should have been here."

Nick released her. "I'm here now. I had other resort business I was working on."

For the first time since he arrived, she noted a sadness in his eyes. But more than that, there was a determination layered with the pain. Wherever he'd been, it hadn't been with a date.

And maybe she had let her imagination run rampant with thoughts of him being with another woman while she cleaned up this mess. She was irritable and stressed, but that was no excuse.

"I'm sorry," she told him. "I don't like accidents and I don't like injured employees, especially because this one seems shady. The firm won't like any of this at all, but the incident was out of my control, and the crew member was here alone when he shouldn't have been here to begin with."

"Don't apologize to me," Nick commanded. "And your firm won't blame you. It's not your fault the guy couldn't do his job properly. He's fired as far as I'm concerned."

Silvia nodded, turning her attention back to the hole that opened up to the basement. "The foreman already suspended him without pay until we could further assess the situation."

As she walked Nick through the events, he listened without chiming in, and she noted that he looked at her when she spoke. His eyes held on to hers like every word that came out of her mouth mattered. He wasn't trying to figure things out or looking around to get his own read on things. He was taking her opinion seriously, listening to her story and respecting her as the architect on the project.

The air seemed thick, almost sticky as she kept talking. Silvia found herself dabbing the sweat off her cheeks. The hard hat certainly didn't help. When black spots danced in front of her face, Silvia closed her eyes a moment and pulled in a deep breath. None of that helped, either. The heat or the altitude must really be getting to her.

The next thing she knew, her world tipped, and strong arms banded around her a second before she was hauled against a broad, firm chest.

"Silvia?"

Nick's worried tone had her wanting to reply, but she couldn't find the energy. What was wrong with her? She felt…she couldn't find the word, but she was hot and sweaty and her body just seemed to lose energy all of a sudden.

As Nick carried her over to the windowsill and sat her down, her hard hat fell to the floor with a thunk.

Silvia started to open her eyes, but a wave of nausea swept over her once again.

"Just…give me a minute," she murmured, gripping his shoulders.

His hands roamed over her, then framed her face. "You're clammy and pale. I'm taking you to the emergency room."

"No." She opened her eyes slowly to focus on his worried gaze. "They're only going to tell you I'm pregnant."

"What if something else is wrong?" he asked, his eyes searching hers. "I don't know anything about this, but I don't want to take chances, because I'm out of my element here."

Even though the room wasn't spinning, Silvia still felt more sluggish than she ever had before. She pulled in a deep breath and pressed her hands to Nick's chest.

"Give me some space," she told him. "I'm fine. I just need air."

Nick came to his feet and continued to stare down at her. Those bright blues roamed all over her face.

"What all have you done today?" he asked, clearly trying to figure out what had happened. "Maybe you overdid it."

"I had a 9:00 a.m. meeting, then I worked on restructuring the lobby here. I know you said it was fine, but I still feel like something is off. Maybe it's the archway, maybe that's too feminine? I don't know. I've drawn so many different—"

"Focus," he ordered, smoothing her hair away from her face. "What happened after you were working on the design—which is fine, by the way."

"In the middle of my work at the office, your chair came," she went on. "After all of that, I had another meeting, because my six-month review with the board was this afternoon."

She replayed the review in her mind, the fact that she'd been told she was doing well enough with the Campbell project, but they'd like her to take on more projects and really push harder.

She was already doing more than several of the male associates at her level. Just wait until she informed them she would be taking maternity leave. She really had no clue what to expect at the end of that conversation.

"Oh, when I came home I found your other surprise," she told him. "That was certainly not necessary, but thanks."

"Did you eat?" he asked.

Silvia shook her head. "I had just put it all away when I got the call about the injury here."

"So you haven't had dinner. What time did you have lunch?"

She shrugged. "I didn't get out for lunch, but I had an apple and a granola bar at my desk around eleven."

Nick cursed under his breath. "You can't do that. Skipping meals or half-assing them may have worked in the past, but our baby needs more than a few hundred calories."

Silvia squared her shoulders and came to her feet, proud of herself for only swaying slightly. "I am well aware of how to care for myself and the baby. I got busy. I would've had a normal meal, but I got called here…when they couldn't get in touch with you, by the way."

"I was busy."

His lips thinned, and his eyes narrowed. Silvia propped her hands on her hips and snorted.

"Too busy to check your phone? I know you had it with you."

"My private life is none of your concern," he tossed back.

The jab shouldn't sting—after all, they didn't have a commitment to each other—but that didn't stop the piercing pain. The implication that she wasn't important enough for him to share that aspect of his life hit her hard, even though they had agreed to secrecy…to being physical only. Even though those limits had been her own idea.

"That goes both ways," she replied. "I can take care of myself, so the gifts need to stop, and I can get myself home and make my own dinner. I don't need a keeper. Now, if we're done here, I've had a long day."

Silvia turned and scooped up her hard hat and gathered her purse and phone. Nick's heavy stare remained on her, but she ignored him. Any other man would argue with her or apologize or stop her or *something*. But no. He just stood there staring in that infuriating way, and she used all her willpower not to throw her hard hat at him.

"Are you okay to drive?" he finally asked, his tone low and uneasy.

Silvia glanced over her shoulder and nodded. "Don't worry about me. You might want to check on your injured worker, though, and get to the bottom of what really happened."

She didn't wait for him to reply before she turned and left him standing in the mess. Besides the report she'd have to write and turn in concerning the injury, she'd also have to work on the new floor. She was only thankful this had happened now and not when they were further along.

Not that she wanted anyone to get hurt, but things could've been so, so much worse. No matter whose fault the accident was, nobody wanted this black mark on their name.

She drove home and cursed herself for being a fool where her feelings and Nick were concerned. The sweet gestures, the way he cared for her—could something deeper be developing here? Hadn't she learned her lesson about letting people in? Being tossed around her entire childhood had proven to her that she could only depend on herself.

And there was still that gaping hole that she'd carried with her for thirty-two years. A hole that only love and stability could fill. She had doubts she'd ever be able to fully seal that void…even if part of her couldn't help but hope she would some day.

Silvia might be angry and hurt by Nick's words, but that wouldn't stop her from devouring the food he'd had delivered. Now, if she could figure out what to do with her attraction to him. Because no matter how upset she was, she still felt a pull toward him that had nothing to do with the baby and everything to do with the fact that her body could still feel his touch. Being near him every day only put her even more on edge.

And she could barely admit this to even herself, but when he was near, that gaping hollowness in her life seemed to lessen.

So what would happen if she let him fill that void? Would the day come when Nick would ultimately crush her heart?

Nick shot off the text to the mayor, inviting him to a special meeting at Hawkins Distillery. Nick and Sam were working from all angles, and getting the mayor alone, away from Rusty or any other influencers, would be key in making this alliance work.

He gripped his cell and stared out the windshield

at Silvia's mountainside home. He'd finally gotten her address, a necessary move since they had leapt from coworkers to one-night-stand to parenthood. They couldn't keep hiding their personal lives forever.

The beautiful stone-and-log house seemed to be lit up all over. Windows encompassed the entire side addition, and the second-story peak had a glow beaming from the accent window as well. The old-fashioned lanterns flanking the front door seemed inviting, but he wasn't so sure she'd welcome him in.

He deserved to have the door slammed in his face. He deserved her anger. He was here to take all of that. Whatever she needed to do so they could move on, he would accept.

Nick stepped from his truck. He'd hurt her earlier. It wasn't her fault his entire world was turned in all directions, but he'd lashed out at her like she was the problem.

How was he honoring his mother's memory if he treated Silvia like she didn't matter? One thing he'd loved most about his mother was her ability to make everyone happy, to make everyone feel special.

And Silvia did matter. Damn it, he just wished she didn't matter so much.

Nick wasn't surprised when the front door opened as he stepped onto the stone porch. Silvia had changed into a pair of leggings and an off-the-shoulder tee that was probably meant for comfort, but she looked sexy as hell. In the few months he'd known her, Nick had never been turned off. Everything about this woman kicked him in the hormones, making him feel things he didn't even know existed. She could rock a suit like the badass businesswoman she was and then transform into the girl next door with those bright blue eyes and wild red hair.

Ignoring all the ways she tugged at his heart was becoming more and more difficult.

Nick kept telling himself he was just too vulnerable right now, with his mother being sick and then her passing. Combine that with the news about the pregnancy, and that's the only reasoning that could explain the constant, invisible tug he felt toward Silvia.

"Come to apologize?" she asked, blocking the door.

Nick nodded. "I did."

"Then you can come in."

He had to hide his smile at her bold, matter-of-fact greeting. This firecracker was surely going to be the one who pushed him over the edge…and he couldn't quite decide if that was a good thing or not.

Silvia turned back into the house, leaving the door open. He wasn't going to ignore that invitation…or those swaying hips. Nick prided himself on his self-control, but when it came to Silvia, he wondered exactly who held the strings.

As he stepped into the open living area, he closed the door behind him. Everything in this space gave him little glimpses into Silvia's personality and lifestyle. The L-shaped stone island had four leather stools tucked beneath it. A bowl of limes sat on the concrete top…no doubt an even number of produce. Straight ahead were floor-to-ceiling windows that stretched up two stories to allow a magnificent view of the mountainside and valley below. But before that view was a spectacular firepit area and pool.

Her living room had more stone surrounding the statement fireplace. A shaggy white rug covered a good bit of the dark wood floors, and her cozy gray furniture held colorful throw pillows in a variety of patterns. She had a little bit of a playful side thrown in with all of the strong elements.

Silvia bustled around in the kitchen, putting things back into the fridge and wiping off her counter. Nick took a seat at one of the stools and rested his arms on the island.

"I was a jerk earlier," he started.

"Yes."

He bit the inside of his cheek to keep from grinning. She wouldn't make this easy, and perhaps that was part of her appeal. She didn't shrink away from challenges or just accept all that happened around her. She took charge while maintaining her dignity. He was positive she'd wanted to throat punch him earlier.

"I don't know how to treat this…whatever is going on between us," he admitted. "You want things kept quiet about the baby, about us. Part of that irks me, but I get it. I do. But I also have some personal issues that I can't talk about yet."

Or ever. Coming to grips with the fact that Rusty was most likely his father was one thing, but sharing that news with the world was a completely different matter entirely. Nick waited each day for a phone call or for someone to show up at his office or home saying they'd received a letter, too, that they might be his half brother. Or should he seek them out? Did he really want to overturn their lives as well?

Did Rusty know any of this even existed?

According to the letter, he knew he was going to be a father, but Nick highly doubted Rusty knew who his son was…or if he did, then he simply didn't care. Nick wasn't going to discount any possibility. At this point, nothing would surprise him.

To say he was on edge was a vast understatement.

"We're both in unfamiliar territory and trying to push through," she told him as she folded her dishrag in a neat rectangle and draped it over her sink. "But you can just say you can't talk about what's bothering you without being a jerk, and I would understand. I'm not asking for a commitment from you or even exclusivity. I mean, I realize you probably want to date and see other women. You shouldn't be tied to me just because—"

Nick was up and around the island before he even realized he'd moved. Her words died as he caged her in and hovered his mouth near hers.

"Exclusivity?" he growled. "Maybe that's exactly what I want. Maybe I hate sneaking around when I actually want to see you outside of work and behind closed doors."

Which he hadn't even realized he wanted until now. What the hell was happening to him?

"What?" she gasped. "No. That would be a *relationship*. We aren't doing that. Just because I'm pregnant doesn't make *us* a good idea. Neither of us is cut out for long-term, and we hardly know each other on a personal level."

Damn her for being logical when he wanted more. More what, though, he wasn't sure.

"I'm not saying that because you're pregnant," he retorted. "I'm saying it because I want to see more of you, not work related, and not always in the bedroom."

Her eyes widened, then her brows drew in. "But we're not those people. We don't do relationships. I… I can't."

Something in her tone sounded downright terrified, and every part of Nick wanted to push her to tell him why. He wanted to know those nuggets of information that all came together to make up who she was today.

"I was married once," he blurted out. Maybe if he opened up a little, she would feel more at ease to do the same. "It didn't last long."

Realizing he was still hovering over her, Nick took a step back and shoved his hands in his pockets.

Maybe that failed marriage was just another example of why he shouldn't mess with Silvia's feelings. Who was he to ask for more? Just look at who his biological father was. Nick had Russ's blood in his veins. Could he ever really be what she wanted, what she deserved?

Even so, he continued.

"We married right out of high school," he stated. Silvia's eyes remained locked on his, so he kept going, hoping she would see just how serious he was about wanting to share with her. "We were in serious lust, but neither of us knew what love meant. I'm not sure I do now, either, but that's beside the point. Her father was livid about us, which only made me want her more."

Silvia smiled. "I could see that. What was her name?"

"Molly. We realized our mistake about two months in. We ignored it, though, because we were both so headstrong and wanted to prove her parents wrong."

"What did your mother think?"

Nick laughed. "She told me I was too young to marry, but she would support any decision I made. She always had my back."

And with that support system gone, now that he needed her more than ever, he was fumbling through his days, his life, trying to find the proper balance.

"So when did you divorce?" Silvia asked.

"We were married six months. We parted on good

"One Minute" Survey

You get TWO books
and TWO Mystery Gifts...

See inside for details.

Dear Reader,

Your opinions are important to us. So if you'll participate in our fast and free "One Minute" Survey, **YOU** can pick two wonderful books that **WE** pay for!

As a leading publisher of women's fiction, we'd love to hear from you. That's why we promise to reward you for completing our survey.

IMPORTANT: Please complete the survey and return it. We'll send your Free Books and Free Mystery Gifts right away. **And we pay for shipping and handling too!**

Thank you again for participating in our "One Minute" Survey. It really takes just a minute (or less) to complete the survey… and your free books and gifts will be well worth it!

↖ *We pay for EVERYTHIN*

Sincerely,

Pam Powers

Pam Powers
for Reader Service

"One Minute" Survey

GET YOUR FREE BOOKS AND FREE GIFTS!

✓ Complete this Survey ✓ Return this survey

1 Do you try to find time to read every day?
☐ YES ☐ NO

2 Do you prefer stories with happy endings?
☐ YES ☐ NO

3 Do you enjoy having books delivered to your home?
☐ YES ☐ NO

4 Do you share your favorite books with friends?
☐ YES ☐ NO

YES! I have completed the above "One Minute" Survey. Please send me my Two Free Books and Two Free Mystery Gifts (worth over $20 retail). I understand that I am under no obligation to buy anything, as explained on the back of this card.

225/326 HDL GNNS

FIRST NAME	LAST NAME

ADDRESS

APT.#	CITY

STATE/PROV.	ZIP/POSTAL CODE

READER SERVICE—here's how it works:

▲ If offer card is missing write to: Reader Service, P.O. Box 1341, Buffalo, NY 14240-8531 or visit www.ReaderService.com ▲

BUSINESS REPLY MAIL
FIRST-CLASS MAIL   PERMIT NO. 717   BUFFALO, NY

POSTAGE WILL BE PAID BY ADDRESSEE

READER SERVICE
PO BOX 1341
BUFFALO NY 14240-8571

NO POSTAGE
NECESSARY
IF MAILED
IN THE
UNITED STATES

terms, and she's actually remarried now with four kids."

"Four?" Silvia laughed. "Sounds like maybe you two weren't compatible. I can't imagine you coaching a ball team or schmoozing with parents in the school pickup line."

Nick hadn't even thought of that. Maybe he wouldn't be that kind of parent. He had no clue, but he did know he wanted this child…and for the time being, he wanted Silvia. Who knew what the future held? Life was fleeting, and if he wanted something, he had to take action and not wait.

"I wasn't ready for marriage or a child when we were married."

"And now?"

"Are you proposing?" he asked, smiling.

Silvia jerked, her face scrunched. "Not at all. I'm not marrying now, if ever."

"You have something against marriage?"

She sighed. "I did it once. It lasted about as long as yours, so I'm definitely not looking for a repeat. I learn from my mistakes."

Interesting. The more they chatted, the more he discovered about her, the more he realized they were similar. Every layer he peeled back revealed something else remarkable that showcased her strength and perseverance.

How many more similarities would he uncover before the lines of their lives ultimately intertwined?

Nine

Silvia didn't know how they'd ended up out back with a crackling fire, cozied up with a blanket, sitting in the same oversize lounger. One minute they were sharing pieces of their past, and the next, she was giving him a tour and he'd fallen in love with the outdoor living area…so here they were.

"I'd never leave this spot if I lived here," he told her.

"You have a pretty awesome place yourself," she retorted.

Silvia stretched out her legs and crossed her ankles, trying desperately not to brush against him any more than necessary. Then again, she didn't need to touch him to be utterly turned on and ready to rip his clothes off.

But she tried to stay in control of the situation and not act like a teenager with a crush.

"This view is what sold me on the place," she admitted. "All of the windows on the back of the house and this firepit area, the pool, didn't hurt, either. I've only been here six months, so I missed the autumn leaves. I can't wait to see all the colors this fall. This is the perfect place to grab a sweatshirt and cuddle next to a fire with s'mores. Oh, maybe I need an outdoor rocker—you know, for the baby?"

"This is a great home for raising a child," he told her.

Silvia smiled. "It is. I've already decorated the spare room a hundred times in my head."

Nick shifted, turning toward her. "You're feeling okay now?"

She glanced his way, then back to the flames licking the darkness. "I'm fine. I just needed to eat. The day got away from me, but I promise to be more aware. I'm still getting in the mind-set that I'm not the only one I need to look out for anymore."

Nick slid his hand beneath the thick blanket and covered her flat belly. Silvia tensed, her eyes darting to his, and she found him solely focused on her.

"I respect your independence, but you have to know that I'm going to worry and I'm going to be pushy and I will likely piss you off. It has nothing to do with not thinking you can't do this alone and everything to do with the fact that you don't have to."

Silvia swallowed, unable to form words. Between

his comforting touch and intense stare and gravelly voice, Silvia couldn't concentrate. Nick possessed every single quality she didn't want to want. He said and did all the right things…but opening herself to the possibility of hurt was not something she could ever do again.

Neither of them was in a position to make life-altering decisions right now, either. They had a baby to think about, and she had to keep that in the forefront of her mind. She would never allow a child in her care, especially her own, to ever feel unwanted or second best. This baby had to be the top priority, above her wants and dreams and desires, above her fears.

"What are we doing here?" she finally asked, holding his gaze.

"Enjoying the nice evening."

She slid her hand over his and removed it from her stomach. "You know what I mean. I don't want a relationship. And you…well, you're not ready, either."

"Maybe not," he agreed. "Does that mean we can't just go out and enjoy our time together? We get along, Silvia. That's rare these days. I would think that's something you understand more than anybody."

Silvia settled onto her back and stared up at the starry sky. She wished she had all the answers; she wished she had someone she trusted enough to tell all her problems to and seek advice. But she'd been a loner her entire life. She really was used to this empty feeling…she just didn't like it.

"I can't let you in," she finally said. "I have nothing to offer, and anything I do have will go to the baby."

Nick sat up and turned, hovering over her so she was forced to look directly into his eyes. "I have never asked for anything. And I won't."

"You can't promise that."

His silence said more than any words could.

"I get the attraction," she added. "That's difficult to ignore. But we have to accept that it's just temporary."

"Temporary," he repeated, like she'd just offended him. "Because you want to keep me your dirty little secret so your coworkers don't know you slept with me? Fine. Keep me your secret, but for now… keep me."

His lips touched hers almost before she realized he was leaning in. Instant arousal assaulted her, and Silvia arched into that strong, firm body. Everything about Nick pulled her in. No amount of self-talk and mental prepping could hold against such a potent man.

One hand gripped her thigh and the other flattened against the lounger beside her head as he held himself above her.

Nick's lips traveled from her mouth, across her jawline and over her exposed shoulder. Anticipation pumped through her, but she'd known where this would lead. Sex was what they knew, a language they both understood in a time when they were both so confused and emotionally torn.

"However long this lasts," he murmured against her skin, "just let it."

How could she argue with his logic? They both wanted this physical connection; they craved it. Maybe they were using each other to combat all the hurt that had built up in their lives. Whatever the reason, there was no way she could deny either of them this moment…and likely the next one, too.

Nick eased back and stared down at her. With her sole focus on him, Silvia reached for the hem of her tee and pulled it up over her head, tossing it aside without a care. His eyes raked over her, and that heavy-lidded stare was just as potent as his touch.

If he weren't a client, she might be brave enough to put aside her fears and dive headfirst into this unknown territory. But he was, and that was all the reason she needed to keep him at arm's length. She'd worked too hard to get to where she was. Sex she could handle. Sharing custody she could handle. Letting her heart get involved would certainly push her over the edge.

"I don't want to pressure you," he added.

Silvia reached for his shirt, keeping her eyes locked on his. "Do I look like I'm being pressured?"

With a sly grin, he helped her pull off his shirt. In a flurry of hands and laughter, they removed the rest of their clothes, leaving everything in piles dotting the patio.

"I guess this is just a perk of living on a secluded mountainside," she told him as he settled between her legs.

"One of many."

Nick's strong hands held on to the back of her thighs as he barely touched their bodies together. Silvia tensed, waiting for that connection, aching enough that a moan of desire escaped her.

But he didn't merge their bodies; he simply stared at her with one brow quirked.

Silvia nodded. "Do it."

Nick eased into her, and Silvia gasped as her body bowed. He didn't take his time; he didn't slow this down. No, Nick jerked his body against hers as he braced his hands on either side of her. Silvia reached for him, but in the next move he had shifted both of them to his side of the lounger, and she straddled his lap. He moved quickly, but clearly he knew what he wanted.

Silvia curled her fingers around his shoulders as she continued the frantic pace. Every nerve ending in her sizzled with an ache that only Nick could satisfy. His hands cupped her breasts as he tipped his head to capture her mouth once again.

The man kissed with such passion, making her feel every bit of his need. Silvia rose up just a tad, then eased back down, pulling out a long, low groan from Nick. She wanted to make him lose his mind here. She wanted to be the one he fantasized about, the one he couldn't get enough of. For reasons she was too frightened to explain, she wanted to be his everything.

But, since that was an unobtainable dream, she was going to take what he offered temporarily. She deserved every bit of happiness she could hold on to.

The battle she kept waging with herself over Nick and how far she wanted to let this go would have to wait. She just needed to be in this moment, absorbing all the pleasure he was willing to give.

When Nick released her lips and covered one breast with his mouth, Silvia threaded her fingers through his hair and allowed herself to be utterly consumed by Nick's touch, his passion.

The crisp night air washed over her bare body, only adding to the overwhelming sensations. There was something so free, so delicious about being out in the open and completely exposed. She didn't want this to end, but her body climbed to the peak and there was no holding back the euphoric burst.

Silvia cried out just as Nick slid one hand between them to touch her where they were joined. His hips bucked beneath hers as his entire body tensed. Silvia dropped her head back, taking in every bit of their climax.

Nick's lips slid up the valley between her breasts, and Silvia focused her attention back to the top of his head. He mumbled something against her heated skin, but she couldn't enjoy the afterglow *and* decipher words right now.

She finally stopped trembling, and Nick wrapped his arms around her and gathered her against him. Silvia rested her head in the crook of his neck, inhaling his musk and woodsy cologne.

"Let me stay," he murmured. "We have nowhere to be tomorrow."

She should make him leave. She should try to keep some kind of line drawn in this confusing relationship, but she couldn't ignore one very important fact.

Her heart was becoming involved in this entanglement—and she worried she wouldn't be able to prevent another heartache.

Silvia woke to the robust aroma of dark roast. She blinked against the sunlight streaming in through her windows. She'd never slept long enough to be awakened with the bright natural light, so she tapped her phone to see the time.

The sudden movement and the combined scent of coffee and something cooking in the kitchen had her stomach instantly revolting.

She tore off the covers and dashed to her en suite bathroom just in time. Sweat dampened her forehead, and a wave of heat overcame her. Stripping off Nick's T-shirt, which she'd slept in, Silvia welcomed the coolness of the bathroom floor tile.

When she felt confident enough that she wasn't going to be sick again, she sank back on her heels and closed her eyes. Silvia pulled in a deep breath and concentrated on her breathing and waited for the rest of the queasiness to pass. Something would have to be done about those smells.

With a groan, Silvia started to get up, but her legs were weak and she was pretty sure the room was spinning again. She closed her eyes just as heavy footsteps sounded down the hall and entered the bedroom.

Not the morning-after look she'd been going for, but there wasn't much she could do about that now. Apparently, morning sickness was ready to make an appearance at this stage of her pregnancy.

"Silvia." Nick rounded the door frame and stilled. "What can I do?"

She held on to the edge of the sink and shook her head. "Nothing. It will pass, but whatever you're making has to go. I'm sorry."

"Consider it done."

He disappeared, and she was thankful he didn't hang around and insist on helping her. She really wanted to wash her face and brush her teeth alone, and if she was going to get sick again, she truly didn't want an audience.

Thankfully, he left her alone, and Silvia managed to grab a quick shower.

Once she was feeling somewhat human again, Silvia tugged his T-shirt back on and pulled her hair up on top of her head. Silvia padded out into the living area and found her doors and windows open and no sign of the food.

Nick rested a hip against the island and held a cup of coffee. "Water or juice?"

"I can get it," she told him as she moved into the kitchen. "What had you made?"

"French toast. It's in the trash, and I took it outside."

Her stomach grumbled, but there was no way she could put anything heavy in there right now. She reached for the bread and popped a slice in the toaster. Bland and blah would likely become her new diet for the foreseeable future.

"I appreciate you making me breakfast," she told him as she turned to face him. "But listen—"

"Regrets already?" he asked, taking a sip of his coffee like he hadn't a care in the world. "I really thought we were past that."

Silvia gritted her teeth. "No, not regrets. I just think we need to not kid ourselves and think that we can play house."

"I'm not playing at anything." Nick set his cup on the island and started moving toward her. "If you're afraid of these emotions, that's understandable, but don't tell me what we're doing is wrong."

"But it is," she countered. "I'm confused because

I want you, but I don't *want* to want you…if that makes sense."

"You're not going to get hurt," he assured her.

Silvia placed a hand on his chest to stop him from coming any closer as she met his gaze. "But what if I hurt you?"

"I've been hurt before." He curled his fingers around her wrist and removed her hand, then laced their fingers together. "We both have experienced divorce and loss, and look at us. We're pushing through. Nothing can keep us down. Are you really afraid to give this a try with me?"

She studied his eyes as his words settled in. "Why do you want this so much?"

Nick's lips thinned, and his jaw clenched before he spoke. "Because I saw my mother struggle. I saw her try to be two parents at one time. I don't want that for you, and if the two of us can see how we are together, if we could make something work, that will only help the baby."

The baby.

Nothing to do with how he felt about *her*.

Oh, he enjoyed the sex, obviously, but was there anything beyond the physical? Surely he had some inkling of emotion for her or he wouldn't keep going to all of this trouble to be with her, to please her.

But…everything he'd done circled back to what was best for Silvia as a pregnant woman, not Silvia as a woman who was growing much too attached to Nick.

"I'm on board with keeping this just between us," he went on. "But don't push me aside before we have a chance to see if this is the right move."

For the baby.

The words hovered between them just the same as if he'd said them.

But hadn't she wanted them to have emotional distance? Hadn't she thought that would feel safer?

And didn't she want him, temporarily?

Maybe, if it was all about the baby, they *could* try this out, without any heartbreak. She just had to keep her heart protected at all costs.

There had to be some ground rules, though. If he was going to continue to be sweet and open and sexy, then she'd have to have some boundaries—that was the only way to ensure she wouldn't get hurt.

"No more gifts."

Nick nodded.

"No more meals."

He quirked a brow. "I have to eat, too."

She didn't hide her smile. "Then no more meals delivered to my house."

He nodded his agreement. "Anything else?"

"Yeah. If you want to end this, tell me. But until then, this is just physical and completely behind closed doors."

Nick pulled in a deep breath and held up a hand, but she put a finger over his lips.

"That's the deal."

His eyes held hers a moment before he ultimately nodded.

There. At least she would retain some control, and hopefully, if fate was on her side, she wouldn't endure any more heartache.

Ten

Nick pulled into the parking space marked "VIP" and chuckled. Like hell would he be a VIP member of Lockwood Lightning. But he wanted to be petty, and he wasn't apologizing. After all, wasn't he technically heir to this hillbilly dynasty?

Did he have a meeting scheduled with Rusty? No. Did he want to be here? Also no. Did he want to see the man squirm? Oh, hell yeah.

Catching the enemy with the element of surprise was just one of the tools in Nick's arsenal. After the card game the other night, Nick figured stopping in to headquarters was the perfect opportunity to talk to Rusty and keep the old man on his toes. Nick wanted Rusty to be wondering what would happen next. Nothing like an impromptu Monday morning meeting to really catch your nemesis off guard.

Nick slid his hands into his pockets and whistled as he crossed the lot to the back offices. He wasn't completely sure of what he'd say once he got in there, but he wasn't concerned. Nick had come to accept that he'd have to take each day, each moment, one at a time and decide his direction once he was in the moment.

The old two-story brick building sat next to the creek that ran through the back of the property, just like Hawkins. Nick stepped into the main entrance and walked right up to the receptionist. He was hoping for a young lady, but there was a middle-aged man. Okay, fine. He could work with that.

As Nick crossed the open lobby, and the guy glanced up from his computer. "Can I help you?"

"I'm here to see Rusty."

The man glanced back to the computer, clicked a few keys, and looked back to Nick. "What was your name?"

"Nick Campbell."

He had to give the man credit. He only slightly cringed at Nick's introduction. His reputation must have preceded him. Now what had dear old dad been saying about him?

"I don't have you down for an appointment this morning."

"This is a pressing family matter," Nick replied

with a smile. "I'm sure Rusty would much rather meet me in private than for me to discuss it here with you or take it to social media."

Okay, so the "family matter" description was a slip, but whatever. Nick could gloss that over later.

"Is that a threat?" the man asked.

The door behind Nick opened, but he paid no attention to whoever came in. He merely tucked his thumbs in his belt loops and shrugged.

"More of a promise," he stated with a wide grin. "Trust me. Rusty would rather we talk in private, and I'm not leaving until we do."

Nick felt someone standing behind him, so he glanced over his shoulder and was greeted with a nervous smile from a twenty-something blonde.

He shifted his focus back to the receptionist. "As I was saying, I can be out of your way in seconds. Just point me toward Rusty's office."

"Security is one call away."

Nick nodded. "They are, but I don't think Rusty would appreciate that. Things will be much better for him if I speak to him. Now."

The guy wanted to argue, Nick could see it plain as day. So Nick didn't move, didn't even blink. He stared back and dared the man to pick up that phone.

Ultimately, the man nodded. "Up the stairs and to your left. The door at the end of the hall."

Nick smiled. "Have a good day."

Mounting the stairs, Nick ignored the nerves curling through him and focused on the sole reason for this visit—his mother. She would want him to see this through. She would want him to fight for what was right. And, really, this push against Rusty went well beyond just trying to serve hard liquor in Nick's new resort. He was doing all of this because Rusty kept his dirty hands in the pockets of the city council and any powerhouse who could benefit him, and Nick was tired of Rusty being a damn bully.

There were plenty of high-class restaurants in Green Valley, but unless Rusty owned them, the establishments didn't have the authority to sell liquor. Rusty wanted to monopolize the multimillion-dollar industry, and Nick wasn't going to just sit back like others had done. He would fight Rusty until the old man either gave in or gave up. Nick had motivation, youth and more money than that old bastard. And money did talk, quite loudly.

Nick reached the wide double doors at one end of the long hall. There were a few offices at the other end, but other than that, this second floor was rather quiet. Nick couldn't imagine working for Rusty— just the thought was a nightmare.

Being the man's son was worse, but only if Rusty found out the truth. Nick had to assume the old man would try to use it against Nick.

Nick didn't bother knocking—no doubt the minion downstairs had already called up to give a report.

He eased the door open. Rusty stood facing the windows overlooking the back of the property.

"You must really want to see me, to bust into my card game and bully your way into my office."

Nick took that as his invitation to come in. He closed the door at his back and crossed the spacious office. Rusty glanced over his shoulder as Nick came to stand on the other side of the wide desk.

"What's it going to take to get you to release your hold on the council members so they will allow a liquor permit for my resort?"

With a gruff laugh, Rusty turned to face him. "I don't have a hold on anybody. They just know a smart business move when they see one, and I happen to have tapped in to the licensing first. Maturity and experience speaks volumes."

So did money and power…both of which Nick had a vast amount over Rusty.

Nick crossed his arms over his chest and adjusted his stance. "Fine, but that their business decisions were made decades ago, and you're no longer the sole distiller in the area. Moonshine is a far cry from bourbon. There's plenty of business to go around."

Rusty stared back, his bushy brows drawn, the buttons straining against the material over his protruding gut. Just when Nick began to wonder if he'd have to repeat himself, Rusty let out a snort.

"You came all the way here to have this same conversation?" Rusty asked, curling his old, chubby fingers around the back of his desk chair. "You wasted your time and mine."

"You won't win this fight," Nick retorted. "You *can't* win it. You might as well make things easier on yourself and just cooperate. Do the right thing for once, or you could regret it."

Rusty raised his busy brows. "Is that a threat?"

Nick dropped his hands and shrugged. "Take it how you want, but you're smart enough to know a formidable opponent when you see one."

"You are nothing to me," Rusty said. "You can't touch me, but watching you try is rather entertaining."

Nothing to him?

If he only knew.

Would the truth even make a difference to him? Would Rusty thaw his cold heart if he knew he had a son? Three sons, if his mother was correct?

Nick stared at the evil man and didn't see one shred of resemblance between them, but he had no doubt his mother had told the truth. She had nothing to gain by revealing the secret after her death. And while Nick wanted to know who his half brothers were, he didn't want to disrupt their lives, and he sure as hell didn't want to take time away from bringing Rusty down and getting that license.

"Entertaining," Nick murmured. "Do you know what will be entertaining? When I reveal the dirt I have on you to your cronies. When I clue them in on what a worthless, selfish bastard you really are."

"What dirt? You know nothing about me."

Nick laughed. "The *facts* and evidence I have on you are something you don't want spread publicly, trust me. Everyone has skeletons, Lockwood. You just have to decide who gets to see yours."

Rusty's eyes narrowed as he stepped around his desk. Nick held his ground. Nothing about this man intimidated him. If he hadn't sold moonshine on the black market before it was legalized, he wouldn't have become a millionaire and he wouldn't have opened this distillery. There was nothing glamorous about the history of white lightning and nothing classy about Rusty Lockwood.

"If you have something on me, let's hear it." Rusty came toward him. They stood toe-to-toe, but Nick towered above the man.

"And let you in on my secrets?" Nick shook his head and laughed. "I don't think so. I'd rather you think about what I could possibly have. What would have the potential to bring you down and destroy all you've made for yourself? I'll even be so generous as to give you two weeks to think it over."

Rusty's jaw clenched as his nostrils flared. "You don't come into my business, my office, and threaten me."

Nick smiled and took a step back. "And yet, I just did."

He turned and headed back to the door but stopped and glanced back over his shoulder. "Two weeks,

Rusty. Then your dirty secrets come out for all to enjoy." Nick smiled. "Now that's entertainment."

"The heartbeat is strong, and the baby looks great."

Silvia breathed a sigh of relief. Seeing the image of the baby on the screen made everything seem so real. Hearing the heartbeat had brought a tear to her eye, but she blinked it away.

"How soon until we know the gender?" Nick asked as he stood at her side.

Silvia glanced up at him. "Do you want to find out?"

"If that's okay with you," he replied.

"I actually wanted to wait."

Nick nodded. "Then we'll wait."

He'd insisted on driving her to the ultrasound appointment today. She'd purposely chosen an office thirty minutes outside Green Valley for secrecy's sake.

While she was glad Nick wanted to be involved, there had been something completely off about him since he'd picked her up. He hadn't spoken much, hadn't taken her hand or acted like he was *here*, present in the moment. She didn't know what to expect— they'd agreed they weren't a couple or really in a relationship...mostly because *she* had decided not to go there. Even though they'd discussed rules, there was still no label she was comfortable with putting on whatever was going on here.

But something about him was off.

Once her appointment was finished and she had

her photos in hand, she and Nick stepped into the hallway of the medical complex.

"You want to grab some lunch or something?"

Nick glanced around, then back to her. "I actually need to get to my office. Do you want me to drop you off at your place or the site?"

Disappointment niggled at her. But seriously, this wasn't a date. They weren't going to go grab a nice lunch and discuss baby names and then go back to his house and settle in for a movie and dinner.

"Just take me back to my house," she told him. "I'll get my car."

She didn't know why he'd insisted on driving if he was just going to take her home. Maybe he'd wanted to talk to her about something but didn't know how to bring it up. Maybe he just didn't want to be alone. Or maybe he thought *she* didn't want to be alone. He'd mentioned before that he would be extra protective of her since he'd watched his single mother work so hard. But she didn't want him to just tag along out of obligation. She wanted him to *want* to be here.

Silvia reached out and put a hand on his arm. "You don't have to come to every appointment," she told him. "I know you're busy. That doesn't mean you don't care."

"I am busy, but I'll never be too busy for my child." Those expressive eyes held hers. "And I'm a parent, too. If you're here, so am I."

Okay, well, he left no room for argument. At least

he didn't appear to be one of those fathers who acted like the child was the mother's responsibility.

"Is something going on?" she asked. "You seem… off."

He pulled his key from his pocket and started down the hall toward the parking garage. "I'm fine. Nothing I can't handle."

But he shouldn't have to handle it alone. Wasn't that what he'd been stressing to her? Did he honestly think taking his own advice was a one-way street?

"Maybe if you stopped being so stubborn and actually talked to someone, you would feel better."

He came to such an abrupt halt and she ran into his back.

Nick turned and grabbed her shoulders to steady her.

"Can you take the day off?" he asked.

Silvia blinked and stared, wondering if he was joking. Take the day off? She didn't think a man like Nick even knew what that term meant.

"Um… I probably shouldn't. I already took half a day for this appointment."

Nick nodded, but she saw his excitement vanish.

What had he had in mind? Whatever it was, it had sparked something in him she hadn't seen before.

"I can meet you after work," she suggested, hoping he'd take the olive branch.

"Sure. Yeah. That's fine."

From his tone, she could tell it was anything but fine, and she vowed to find out exactly what was going on with him.

Eleven

Nick stared at his mother's handwriting once again. He had no clue how many times he'd pulled out her letter and read each word. And he didn't really know what he expected to see that he hadn't seen before. Maybe he just wanted to feel that connection with her since this was her final correspondence with him or maybe he just needed to see her handwriting.

Or maybe if he continued to dissect each and every word, he'd figure out her motivation for dropping all of this after keeping the secret for so long.

Nick's cell buzzed with the tone from the front gate. He put the letter back into the safe and pulled his phone from his pocket.

The image of Silvia's SUV filled the screen. He

was surprised she was here, but he typed in the code to open the gate. They'd mentioned meeting up, but that had been the beginning and end of that conversation. He'd dropped her off at her car this morning, and she'd headed off to work. He hadn't spoken to her since.

Nick had been feeling irritated for the past two days, ever since leaving Rusty's office on Monday morning. Every moment that passed without a call from Rusty had Nick twitchy. The last thing he wanted to do was drag the old man through the wringer, because Nick's mother would be in that wringer as well. He had to hope Rusty would cave. There was still time, but with each passing day, Nick became more certain that Rusty was calling him on his bluff.

Nick stepped from his office and headed downstairs to greet Silvia at the door. He owed her an apology yet again. He seemed to be doing that quite a bit lately, but he also hadn't been himself since the funeral. The Nick she'd met months ago wasn't the same man he was today.

He hadn't meant to be cranky with her earlier. It wasn't her fault his father was a bastard, or the bane of his existence, or a maniac who had to be stopped. Nick didn't mind taking on Rusty—Nick just wished he could compartmentalize his emotions. He was having a difficult time concentrating on his responsibility to Silvia and their baby because Rusty was consuming his thoughts.

Nick opened the front door just as Silvia's SUV pulled into the circular drive. He stood at the edge of the porch and waited.

As soon as she exited and rounded her vehicle, Nick took in her change of clothes. Earlier she'd had on a sexy pantsuit, but now she had on a simple sundress with a denim jacket and little boots.

"You're turning all Tennessee on me," he joked.

She glanced down and laughed. "I kind of like this vibe. It's comfortable and trendy."

He didn't know much about trendy, but he did know that Silvia knocked the breath out of him and she looked ridiculously sexy.

"I'm sorry that I couldn't take off work earlier," she told him. "I just… I haven't told anyone about the baby yet, and I really had no excuse I could give. This job is important to me and—"

Nick held up his hand. "I get it. I just had a last minute thought. No big deal."

She tipped her head to the side, sending her hair falling over her shoulder. "What was your idea?"

His sour mood instantly switched. There was no reason they couldn't do his plan now. In fact, they both needed the escape and the distraction.

Nick offered her a smile and reached for her hand. "Trust me?"

With a tip of her head, she narrowed her eyes. "Does this involve me losing my clothes?"

"That's not what I had in mind, but I can adjust to your plans."

Silvia took his hand and laughed. "Let's go with your plan first and see how the evening progresses."

He helped her up onto the porch and into the house. Keeping her hand in his, he led her through the entry and toward the garage.

"Where are we going?" she asked, glancing around the house. "Your house is ridiculous, by the way."

He glanced over his shoulder and lifted a brow.

She grinned. "In the best way. It's stunning. I haven't gotten a good look at it like I really want to."

"You'll get the grand tour when we come back," he promised. "I've already pictured you naked on that leather couch in front of the fireplace."

She snorted. "Your seduction technique needs a little work."

He pulled her close, close enough to see those navy flecks in her blue eyes. "I'd say my technique is just fine. You're in my arms right now."

"Touché."

Nick escorted her to the garage and assisted her into his SUV. Once they were on their way, she shifted toward him.

"But really, where are we going?"

He gripped the wheel and rounded the sharp curve heading down the mountain. "You don't do well with surprises, do you?"

"I do...when I know what they are."

Nick laughed and reached for her hand.

"That's not a surprise," he countered. "Just enjoy the ride. We'll be there soon."

"The airport?" Silvia asked. "Nick, I can't leave town. I have a job. One that I have to be at tomorrow morning."

Nick laughed as he pulled up and parked in front of a private plane. "I promise you'll be back before you know it."

Silvia stared at the plane, then looked back to Nick. "I thought you were taking me to show me something or to grab a hamburger or... I don't know. I didn't think I was coming to the airport."

Who did that? Who just picked up on a whim and decided to fly out? This was a lifestyle she wasn't used to living. Her wild nights consisted of making sure all her laundry was done.

Nick got out of the vehicle and came around to get her door. "You're not afraid of flying, are you?"

She stepped out and shrugged. "Not sure. I've never done it."

Nick's mouth dropped. "Never?"

Silvia shook her head. "I guess we're about to find out if I love it or hate it."

She looped her arm through his and started toward the plane. "It will all depend on how good our pilot is."

"You're looking at him."

Silvia jerked to a stop and stared back at Nick. "You fly planes, too? Is there anything you're not good at?"

His mouth quirked into a toe-curling grin. "Well, I've never been a parent, so I'm not sure how I'll be there."

Something tugged at her heart. The more they discussed parenting this baby, the more she wondered just how they could keep going with a physical-only relationship. Because each day that passed, each moment she spent with him, pulled her deeper and deeper into his world. She worried she might never want to leave.

Wasn't that how she'd grown up? Trying to fit into other people's worlds? She'd wanted just one area to call her own. One home, one family. Now with Nick, she was seeing the entire package dangling in front of her. The sexy man who fulfilled her every desire, who made her smile, who would be the father of her unborn child. A family of her own was within her grasp… But what if, just like always, she wouldn't be able to capture it?

"Hey. You okay?"

Nick's question pulled her back to the moment. "Fine. Now, let's see if I like this whole flying thing."

He looked like he wanted to question her further, but he slid his hand over the small of her back and escorted her onto the plane. Silvia opted to sit in the cockpit with him as opposed to in the cabin…which was quite posh and impressive. Rich brown leather sofas, a minibar, even a bedroom in the back.

She didn't want to know how many other women he had taken for impromptu airplane rides just to show off his piloting skills. She wanted to think she was special, that there was something happening here beyond a child and beyond just sex.

Foolish, yes, but she couldn't help her feelings.

Nick explained everything he was doing as he started the plane. Several moments later, he was heading toward the runway, flanked by lights. Silvia couldn't help but stare at him. He seemed so at home here. She'd never known this about him. Clearly he had a passion for flying, or he wouldn't own his own plane and know how to pilot it. He muttered to himself about a preflight check and tapped on various controls and gadgets. Who knew how sexy this would be? She already loved flying.

The moment the plane lifted, Silvia's attention turned to the side window. In an instant, the airport got smaller, the roads were just mere lines and there were lights everywhere. The orange glow from the sunset seemed to light up the world.

"This is gorgeous," she exclaimed, her eyes darting around to try to take in all of the breathtaking views at once. "Is this what you wanted to show me?"

"No. I had no clue you'd never flown or I would've taken you before now."

"So where are we going?"

He glanced her way and offered her a grin. "Just enjoy the mountain views from above."

As he glanced back to the controls, Silvia took his advice. But she couldn't take her eyes off him. The strong jaw, the glasses and the stubble, the intensity and passion rolling off him. This was a man who knew what he wanted, what he craved. Somehow, she'd slid into that role in his life, and she wondered if she could stay there. Was she so foolish as to hope something long-term could come from this?

Before she knew it, they were landing at another airstrip. Silvia had no clue where they were. She figured they'd been flying for about thirty minutes.

"Can you tell me now?" she asked, once he brought the plane to a stop and shut it down.

Nick reached over and squeezed her hand. "I thought you trusted me."

"With this? Sure."

It was everything else she worried about.

"Silvia—"

She smiled and put her finger over his lips. "Let's not say anything else. Just take me to my surprise."

Worry flashed through his eyes a moment before he took her hand from his mouth and kissed her fingertips. Part of her wished she would've let him talk, but the other part—the damaged part—worried about what he would've said.

Twelve

Nick stared across the tiny booth at Double Down Donuts and watched as Silvia thoroughly enjoyed a honey cruller. When she let out a moan and licked her fingertips, Nick readjusted in his seat to alleviate the uncomfortable war between his anatomy and his zipper.

"Does this surprise meet your approval?" he asked.

Her eyes darted to his as she grabbed her napkin and swiped the glaze off her lips. Shame. He'd been looking forward to removing that himself with his own lips.

"Feel free to surprise me anytime with double donuts."

Nick laughed and reached for his iced coffee. "I

figured you'd appreciate the whole even number factor, especially with donuts."

"You already know me so well."

He was learning each day, and not only about Silvia, but about himself as well. He wanted more, but more of what he didn't know. He did know that he was still in a vortex of confusion. He was wading through a chapter in his life that felt as if someone else was writing it.

"This was my mother's favorite donut shop," he told her, trying to get out of his own head. "I'd bring her here once a week until she got too sick to travel. She loved sweets and she loved to fly, so it was a perfect day for her when we came."

Silvia reached across the table for his free hand. "I'm sorry. Does being here bring up bad memories?"

Lacing his fingers with hers, he leaned down and took a drink, then shook his head. "Not at all. I haven't been here in a few months. It's nice to be back."

"I take it this is the booth you always sat in?" she asked.

"Actually, she would usually want to sit at the bar so she could watch them bake in the back. The owner, Stan, he got to the point he would just invite her into the kitchen. He actually closed the café the day of her funeral, and the entire staff attended her service."

Silvia's eyes welled with tears, and her chin quivered as she bit her lip.

"I didn't tell you that so you'd cry," he said with a laugh, not at her, but because tears made him nervous. "I'm just saying that it's nice to be back here and I'm glad I could share this with you."

And he hadn't been quite sure how he'd feel coming back until he'd walked in the door, but having Silvia at his side was a balm he hadn't realized he needed. She settled something in him, filled a void he hadn't known existed. Not the void from losing his mother. No, Silvia had entered the picture before that.

There was something sexy about her intelligence and business sense. It pulled him deeper. He loved that she was making a name for herself in a mostly male-dominated world. That's exactly the type of mother he wanted for his child…a fearless leader and an independent woman.

"Why are you looking at me like that?" she asked, her brows drawn in.

He pulled her hand to his mouth and kissed her knuckles. "Just wondering how soon we can get back to my place."

Awareness and desire flashed through her eyes. "If I recall, there's a bedroom on that plane."

Could there be a more perfect woman? Their parallel thoughts were just another significant turn on.

"I love how that smart mind of yours works."

Nick couldn't get out of the donut shop fast enough. He grabbed their boxes and tugged at her hand, leading her out to the car he'd driven here, the one he kept at the airport. Silvia laughed as he practically ran with her to the car.

"You think this is funny?" he asked, caging her against the side of the car.

The streetlights cast a warm glow over her features, and he realized he wanted to be the man who kept that smile on her face. He wanted to be the one to put that sparkle in her eyes.

Before he could delve too deeply into his emotions, Nick leaned in to brush his lips across hers. When she sighed and opened for him, Nick devoured her. He settled his hands on her hips, pulling her closer to where he ached most.

Silvia threaded her fingers through his hair, knocking his glasses askew.

Nick eased back, righted his frames and raked his thumb across her damp mouth.

"The plane is waiting," he murmured, more than ready to get her back to Green Valley and show her exactly how much he wanted her.

"Nick. Did you hear me?"

Nick rubbed a hand over the back of his neck and gripped his cell. Silvia had left around ten the night before, after they'd gotten back from their impromptu donut run. He'd been up most of the night trying to put his feelings into perspective, but all he came up with was that where Silvia was concerned, he was damn confused. He wanted the hell out of her.

There was nothing more he could want, nothing more he deserved. But was she seeking that family life she'd never had? Even if he wanted to offer one big, cozy, happy family, Nick feared he wouldn't even know how.

But before he could continue driving himself crazy with his chaotic thoughts, Sam called with some startling, unexpected news.

"Say that again," Nick stated.

"I said there's a rumor that Rusty has been skimming from Milestones," Sam stated. "All the money that his employees donate each year and he claims to match, well, the talk is that he has not only *not* been matching it, he has also been taking the monthly donations."

Nick pushed away from his desk and came to his feet. He turned to stare out the back window and across the mountaintops as far as the eye could see.

"I want to say I'm surprised, but nothing that man does shocks me anymore, even if it's illegal. Rumors have circulated around him for years." Nick sighed as a ball of unwanted emotions formed in his stomach. This crooked bastard was his father. "But the fact that he's stealing from a children's charity is a new low."

Milestones was a charity in Tennessee with the mission of helping children under seventeen who suffered from any handicap, mental or physical. The money funded summer camps and educational programs to target the kids' strengths and give them hope for a better future, regardless of their disability.

"That bastard publicly promotes that he urges his employees to donate and that he'll match any amount they raise each month," Sam added. "He preys on the weak to boost his own ego and reputation. I don't have proof, but I have a reliable source that claims Rusty is being investigated regarding these accusations."

Nick gritted his teeth. Was that why Rusty hadn't returned his call from the other day? Was that why he hadn't given in to what Nick demanded? Maybe Rusty was too preoccupied with attorneys and untangling his web of lies.

What would he need to take that money for? Lockwood Lightning brought in millions each year.

Maybe Rusty had a gambling problem or maybe he was paying off more mistresses who claimed to be pregnant with his baby. Who knew what the real problem was.

No matter what mess Rusty was in, Nick would ultimately get what he wanted. Rusty's issues weren't Nick's, and Nick didn't give a damn what Rusty had gotten messed up in.

"If he's stealing from any charity, I don't care who does his books, that's pretty damn difficult to hide," Nick claimed. "He'll get caught eventually. But we need to keep up the pressure. You up for another card game this weekend?"

"Can't," Sam replied. "I'll be out of town for the next few weeks. I'm acquiring two more restaurants on the East Coast and finalizing renovation plans."

Nick turned from the window and stared down at the monitor showing the security footage from cameras covering various portions of his property. A deer ambled by near his back patio, but other than that, absolutely nothing stirred on this early morning.

"I'll keep on Rusty while you're gone," Nick promised. "Maybe all the pressure will be too much for him and he'll finally relent."

"It would have to be something major for him to loosen his grip on those city council members. That good ol' boys' club goes back decades."

That might be, but Rusty didn't know he had a son. And thanks to his mother's insightful note, Nick knew he wasn't the only Lockwood bastard running around. In a perfect world, all three boys would come together and take down the bullying mogul. But Nick didn't live in a perfect world. He had realism running through his veins.

"Rusty is getting sloppy," Nick argued. "That good ol' boys' club won't last forever, especially when the members see there's more money to be had by opening up the liquor laws to a broader spectrum of entrepreneurs. The more liberal they are with the licenses, the more tourism comes into this area, the more the city council and taxpayers benefit. It's simple math and common sense."

Sam laughed. "Remind me to keep you on my good side."

Another call came through Nick's phone, and he glanced to the screen only to see an unknown name. He couldn't assume the caller was a telemarketer, not in his line of work.

"I need to take another call," Nick said. "I'll be sure to keep you posted while you're gone."

"I'll do the same if I hear any more."

Nick disconnected the call with Sam and took the other.

"Hello?"

"Mr. Campbell?"

"Speaking."

"My name is Gertie. I'm Rusty Lockwood's personal assistant. He wants to meet with you at eleven this morning."

Nick glanced to the antique clock on his desk and noted it was just after nine. Had Rusty come around? Was he ready to talk business? No matter what he wanted, Nick was eager to get there.

"I'll be there at ten thirty," Nick stated, simply out of spite. "I have a meeting later that I can't miss. Thanks for calling."

He disconnected before Gertie could give him another time or argue that only eleven would work. Nick didn't know what Rusty wanted, but he had to believe it had something to do with the liquor license. Not that Nick thought the old man would back down so easily, but Nick was relieved that his bluff had captured Rusty's attention. With this recent rumor about the investigation into the charity, maybe Rusty was ready to relieve some pressure any way he could.

Whatever the reason for this sudden meeting, Nick was more than ready to tackle Rusty—and hopefully he wouldn't have to pull out the daddy card.

Thirteen

Silvia smoothed a hand over her flat belly and pulled in a deep breath. She hadn't gotten sick at work before this morning, but now she couldn't seem to stay out of the restroom.

A tap on the door had her groaning. She wasn't sure it was safe enough to exit, but she could always go to the restroom up on the next floor…she only hoped she could make it that far without getting sick again.

She splashed some water on her face and dabbed her cheeks with the backs of her hands. One glance in the mirror and she realized nothing she did would make her look perky or like she was ready to go back to her desk.

Whatever. She couldn't hide in here forever, no matter how nauseated or weak she felt.

Silvia shoved her hair behind her shoulders and straightened her jacket. As soon as she opened the door, she came face-to-face with Edwin, the office manager, just as he was about to knock again.

"Oh, Silvia." He took a step back to allow her to pass. "Um...are you okay?"

Was she okay? Between getting pregnant from a one-night stand and then developing feelings for a man who would likely never reciprocate them, no, she actually wasn't okay.

"Do you need to go home?" Edwin asked, still studying her face. "The last time I saw a woman this pale and shaky was my wife, when she was pregnant with our son. He's a month old now."

Silvia attempted a smile, though her nerves were even more on edge now. The last thing she needed was some busybody coworker outing her secrets.

"I'll be fine in a bit," she assured him. "My breakfast just isn't agreeing with me."

Understatement, but Edwin seemed to believe her, so she excused herself and made her way toward the elevator. She'd rather hang in the bathroom until she was positive it was safe to sit at her desk and go on about her day.

She turned down the hall, spotting the elevator at the end...but her boss stepped right in front of her, blocking her path.

"Silvia."

Clark's voice seemed to boom, which irritated her. She just wanted some privacy and a commode. Was that too much to ask?

"I stopped by your office and couldn't find you," he went on. "I know there was an accident at the Campbell project. I wanted to know what was going on with that claim or if the client had everything settled."

Silvia pressed a hand to her stomach. "My client opted not to file a claim, and the worker who was injured is fine. He was honest about his negligence and has been released from the project."

Clark nodded, seemingly fine with her response. "That's good to hear. I was concerned this would reflect badly on the company, but you handled it like a pro. You're really fitting in quite well here. I see a permanent spot for you, possibly a promotion. We like employees who are determined and focused. The way you put the job first and foremost in your life tells me you're serious about being here and taking on more responsibility."

Silvia's smile widened, though guilt about her secret weighed heavily. She knew that being a mother in this male-dominated office would immediately make her look less committed to her role here. "I really appreciate that. Working at this firm has been a dream come true for me."

"Keep up the good work," Clark praised.

He stepped around her, and Silvia continued on toward the elevator. She wasn't ready to fill them in on her condition. They were pleased with her work, and they saw how devoted she was. If they thought she was going to put her baby first, which she was, and that she would be taking time off for maternity leave, which she also was, she worried they'd pull her from Nick's project. Though she knew Nick wouldn't let that happen, she didn't want Nick or anyone else to have to come to her defense.

As the elevator doors closed, Silvia shut her eyes and rested her head against the cool metal. She could have a successful career and be the doting mother her baby deserved. There was no reason she couldn't do both. It would just take some juggling and plotting…that's all.

For now, and for the next several months, she had to push through. She had to continue to prove herself within the company. She had to give them no reason to doubt her abilities so that when the time came for her to take maternity leave, they would be begging her to come back. This job meant more now than ever, because she had to be the sole provider for not just herself, but for her baby.

The memory of all of those foster homes she'd rotated in and out of filled her mind. She wanted stability for her baby, which meant she couldn't be distracted or confused by where Nick stood in her life. She had to define their relationship and stick to it.

So where did Nick fall in with her long-term goals?
That was her biggest fear…that maybe he couldn't.

Nick stepped into Rusty's office and closed the
door behind him. Rusty stood at his desk with his
hands in his pockets, clearly expecting Nick.

"Are we ready to put an end to this game you're
playing?" Nick asked in lieu of a traditional greeting.

"I don't play games when it comes to business,"
Rusty countered. "I do, however, want to discuss
what you have on me, or what you think you have."

Nick sighed as he stepped farther into the spacious office. "We've already been through this. I'm
not telling you, and I promise, I have proof. So if
that's why you called me here, you've wasted your
time and mine."

Rusty stared across the space, and Nick didn't
waver or back down. He hadn't come all the way
down here to leave without getting what he wanted
or at least move a step toward that ultimate goal.

Nick wondered if he should allude to the charity. Maybe that's the angle that would work for now.

"If you're in some kind of trouble, maybe you
should just do the right thing for once," Nick added.

Rusty's bushy brows drew in. "What trouble do
you think I'm in?"

Nick laughed and took another step closer. Clearly
Rusty was into playing games by pretending he
didn't know what Nick was talking about. "A man of

your position and immoral compass is always going to be in some type of scandal."

"Scandal? I'm not part of any scandal."

Rusty scoffed like Nick was absurd for even mentioning such a thing...which told Nick all he needed to know. Rusty was worried, and that would go a long way in getting Nick what he wanted. Rusty would be desperate to be seen as an upstanding businessman in light of all that was happening. He would need to do something to redeem himself because no matter how many cronies he had in his back pocket, even they wouldn't be able to stand by him if Rusty was indeed stealing from a children's charity.

"Trouble, then," Nick stated. "So, what do you want from me?"

Rusty's face studied Nick. "You're an arrogant bastard, aren't ya?"

Like father, like son.

Maybe, if he was lucky, that was the one and only thing Nick had received from his biological father.

Nick didn't reply; he simply crossed his arms and waited. Patience was key in gaining everything he wanted. He wondered how much patience he'd have with Silvia—and then he immediately wondered why that thought had popped into his mind. He'd never wanted a family; he'd been just fine married to his career. Now here he was with a baby on the way and rolling into a relationship.

No matter what they said to the contrary, there

was no denying the fact that something neither of them had expected was happening.

And yet he still wanted more.

"I'm not giving up anything," Rusty finally stated. "You want to play with the big boys, then you'll have to show your hand, because I'm calling your bluff."

That's exactly what Nick had been afraid of, but he wasn't about to cave. If he could continue the veiled threats, hopefully Rusty would see that Nick wouldn't be scared off or give up. Not going to happen.

"Then you'll be sorry," Nick fired back. "It's your life and reputation you're gambling with. Either way, I'm going to get what I want. You just have to figure out if you want to give it up quietly, like the upstanding man you think you are, or with a very public scandal. Totally your call."

Rusty didn't say a word. He barely blinked, and Nick knew the man was sweating beneath his cheap suit. The old man might have made millions illegally and then tapped into a billion-dollar industry once laws were changed in his favor, but that didn't alter the truth. Rusty Lockwood was just a criminal with no ethics and still working every illegal angle in an attempt to hoard his money.

"I'm not giving up anything," Rusty growled. "If you don't want to tell me the information you have, then I have to believe you have nothing."

"Then that's your mistake."

Nick was not waiting around to argue any more. Without another word, he turned and left the office, letting the door bang against the wall on his way out. Maybe he would have to give up his secret even though he wasn't quite ready yet.

He would press every other angle first. Revealing his paternity would be a last resort.

Nick made a stop at the florist after he left the office and bought flowers for the two women in his life. He decided to go by the cemetery, since he hadn't been since the funeral. He needed a quiet place to think and wanted to feel closer to his mother.

What would she want him to do? She'd given him this information for a reason, even though she'd known Rusty and Nick had never gotten along. Did she just want Nick to finally know the truth, or did she want him to go to Rusty with what he knew? The cryptic letter produced as many questions as answers. And the longer Nick sat on the bench in front of his mother's grave, the more confused he became. He wasn't finding answers in the silence.

Nick had never felt this alone before. Even though he had hundreds of employees and multiple businesses across the globe, that didn't replace having an inner circle he trusted and could lean on.

It couldn't replace the bond he'd had with his mother.

But he could take comfort from the woman she'd been. His mother had never given up. Until she drew her last breath, she'd loved with all she had and worked toward her dream of owning a beautiful mountain resort.

Nick searched through his heart, his mind, and couldn't come up with one single dream of his own. Oh, he had goals and career aspirations, but an actual dream that he was working toward? Not really.

Beating Rusty, finishing the resort and taking care of his baby were the three main focal points in his life right now. Maybe he'd honor his mother by pursuing a dream, something she would be proud of. Because, even though she was gone, he would work every day to continue her legacy.

Nick came to his feet and traced his fingertip around his mother's name on the stone. "Love you, Mom."

When he turned, Nick swiped the dampness from his eyes and set out to make sure he accomplished everything his mother had started.

Fourteen

After last night, Silvia was surprised she hadn't heard from Nick. Not a call, not a text, nothing. There hadn't even been a professional check-in regarding the resort.

Silvia swung by Mama Jane's and ordered double fried chicken, potatoes, rolls and banana cream pie. It was early enough in the evening that she could surprise Nick and return his sweet gesture from last night. Though, after that heated encounter on the plane, she'd say they were pretty equal.

Still, amazing sex aside, she found she wanted to take care of him, to offer comfort where she could. He was going through so much right now and even if they went nowhere romantically, she wanted to be someone he could count on.

Silvia turned up the steep incline toward Nick's drive and stopped at the gate. She punched the button to announce her arrival and waited. She hoped he was home. That was the drawback to surprises. But if he wasn't, she'd take all this food home and eat really well for the next few days. She still had some leftovers in her fridge from his delivery, but she wanted to have a casual dinner with him tonight.

Finally, the gate slid open, and Silvia eased her car up the mountainside. She curved around each turn until the stone-and-log home came into view. The magnificent structure matched the owner: strong, bold, demanding.

Silvia couldn't ignore the flutter that curled through her belly…one that had nothing to do with nausea and everything to do with the man inside that house. She'd dated over the years, but she never recalled getting schoolgirl giddy over anyone before.

Ridiculous, really, to have these innocent, adolescent feelings when she was expecting the man's baby. A little late for crushes and giggles.

Silvia pulled to a stop in the circular drive right in front of the extended porch. Nick didn't step outside like he had before to greet her, which she found odd. He knew she was here, but perhaps he was busy on a call or something. He did have a life beyond her, and she had to not only remember but also respect that.

Just like she wanted to stay guarded, Nick did as well. He was still hurting from his loss, and Silvia would do well to remember that he could just be seeking comfort from her and nothing more.

Ignoring those weighted thoughts, Silvia gathered the takeout bags and headed up the stamped concrete steps to the front door.

She was trying to figure out how to juggle the sacks when the large double doors opened. Immediately she knew something was wrong. His hair was a mess, his glasses were on top of his head, he had on a fitted black tee—which did amazing things for those sculpted arms and shoulders—and he was barefoot. He seemed at home and relaxed, save for the disheveled hair and the sadness in his eyes.

Similar to what she'd seen the other day when he'd pushed her away.

"Did I interrupt something?" she asked, stopping on the third step.

Nick shook his head and pulled his glasses off. He shoved them in his pocket and came down the steps toward her to take the bags.

"This is fine," he told her. "And if this is dinner from Mama Jane's, then it's even more fine."

Mama Jane's was a little hole in the wall that had been at the foot of the Tennessee mountains for decades. It was a local hangout with the best fried chicken and homemade potatoes she'd ever had in her life.

"Please tell me you got dessert, too," he said as he gestured for her to go ahead of him into the house.

"If you don't like their banana cream pie, then you're wrong."

Nick followed her into the kitchen and started unloading the bags. He didn't say anything as he pulled out plates and drinks and silverware. She watched him carrying everything out to the patio, still in silence. Once she realized he intended to eat out there, she gathered what she could and followed.

When the silence stretched, Silvia couldn't take it another second. If he didn't get whatever this was off his chest, he was only going to grow more miserable, and then where would that leave them?

"Something bothering you?"

He set his plate on the table and moved around to take hers and do the same. Then he pulled out her chair.

"Nothing worth discussing," he told her without looking her in the eye.

An unease came over Silvia, and worry settled in deep. Did he want to tell her he'd met someone? Had he decided this secret relationship wasn't working out? Maybe he was worried about the emotional state he was in right now, or that getting involved was a bad idea.

She couldn't argue with that last one, but her heart didn't know common sense. Her heart only knew what she wanted—and she wanted Nick.

Heartache was inevitable. She knew it. She'd told herself over and over that long-term relationships couldn't stem from a passionate fling, and he'd never given any indication he wanted more. Yet she hadn't been able to stop her feelings from turning serious any more than she could stop the sun from setting.

"You don't seem fine," she pushed, taking a step toward him and ignoring her chair. "You can talk to me, you know. I'm a pretty good sounding board, and you clearly need to get something off your chest."

Nick glanced out toward the mountains and the glowing sun, but she didn't take her eyes off him. The muscles in his jaw clenched, and he gripped the back of the chair.

"This might not be a good night for you to be here," he murmured. "I'm just… I'm not in a good space and I won't be good company."

Ignoring his statement, Silvia took another step, then another until she came to stand right next to him. She covered his hand with hers, and every muscle in his body tensed.

"If you're this upset, this is the perfect night for me to be here."

He turned his attention to her, and the torment in his eyes tore at her heart. He opened his mouth, and she waited for him to let her in on what had hurt him, but he ultimately shook his head and took a seat.

"I'd rather eat."

OK. Shutting her out, yet again. She didn't want

to ignore his pain, but she couldn't make him open up. She couldn't make him understand that she was here for him. No, he had to come to that realization himself.

And somehow Silvia recognized that his issue wasn't really so much about not wanting to share with her. It was more that he didn't want to face this himself, which he'd have to do if he shared it with her. That was all the more reason he needed to open up. Or maybe it was all the more reason for her to snap back to the reality that they weren't in a normal relationship. She wasn't even sure what a normal relationship entailed, but this certainly wasn't it.

He had his own life and she had hers—she'd do well to remember that once they moved on and only had a baby in common, she had to have a solid career. That was the only stability she had, and she would not only maintain it, she would grow that part of her life so she could be the best mother and provider for her baby.

Silvia took a seat, served herself a hearty helping of potatoes and dug in. Might as well push beyond the emotional turmoil and deal with what she could—eating.

"You don't want any chicken?"

Silvia shook her head. "I had a rough day, so I'm afraid to put anything too heavy on my stomach."

His fork clattered to the plate as he stared. "Are you okay? You didn't have to bring me dinner. Damn it. I've been so preoccupied with my own issues, I didn't think to ask how you were doing."

"I'm fine," she assured him.

He was obviously trying to deflect and keep the focus on her when he was the one clearly hiding something. She'd thought they were at least friends. Did he not trust her? If he just didn't want to talk, she could understand it, but if he was keeping her shut out for another reason, that stung a little.

She finished eating and didn't attempt any more conversation. When she was done, she simply picked up her stuff and took it back inside. She was rinsing her plate when strong arms came around her. Nick's head dropped into the crook of her neck, and Silvia shut off the water.

"Be patient with me," he muttered against her skin. "I just don't want to think or talk or worry. Just for tonight."

That raw honesty tugged at her heart. He didn't owe her any explanations…that's not why she had pushed. She genuinely wanted to help him through a difficult time. Because right now, even though she hated to admit it, they only had each other.

Silvia turned in his arms and looped her wet hands around his neck. "Tonight," she agreed and covered his mouth with her own.

Nick lifted her up, and she wrapped her legs around his waist. He carried her and she held on, pouring herself into him, letting him take what he wanted. She didn't care where they went, so long as he didn't let her go.

That mentality is what would wind up breaking her heart, but she didn't want to think about that right now. She didn't want to think at all.

She felt the warm evening air on her skin and knew he'd stepped back outside. He gently laid her on the swinging bed suspended beneath an old oak. Nick shed his clothes as he kept his eyes locked on hers. Silvia's body responded, her ache becoming more than she could bear.

Before he finished undressing, she was working on her own clothes, tossing them wherever, eager to feel his skin against her own.

Nick eased onto the bed beside her, sending it swaying gently in the wind. With a quick grip of her hips, he had her up and straddling his lap. She'd never felt so exposed, not even when they'd had sex in the lounger. Here, they were out in the open, in the dusk with the sun still not quite set, and she was completely vulnerable to Nick's stare.

When he reached up to cup her breasts, Silvia arched into his touch. She leaned forward and braced her hands on either side of his head, then lined up their bodies before easing down on him.

Nick's lips thinned as his jaw tightened, but that dark gaze never wavered from her. The way he looked at her made her feel so empowered, so sexy. How could she not fall for this man when he made her feel things she'd never known were possible? How could she not fall for the man who made her want more of everything he was willing to give?

His vulnerability and raw state only made Silvia want to shield him from any more pain. He needed her, and she'd never had anyone actually *need* anything from her. The realization had her falling even more deeply.

Perhaps they needed to heal each other so they could move on together.

Nick's hands roamed down to the dip in her waist and over the flare of her hips. He held her in place as he jerked his hips rhythmically. Silvia groaned as she absorbed all of his emotions, his strength.

The swing swayed, and Nick's fingertips bit into her. Silvia moved with Nick as she leaned down and slid her lips across his. Her hair curtained them both, and she coaxed his mouth open. Nick's hands cupped her backside as his hips pumped faster. The climax built, and Silvia tore her lips from his as the sensations spiraled through her. She eased back, holding her body upright as she pumped her own hips.

Nick gripped her waist and tensed beneath her as his body bowed and he followed her pleasure. Silvia squeezed her eyes shut, not wanting any of her true feelings to show—not now when she was too vulnerable and on the edge of completely falling in love with Nick Campbell.

When their bodies settled, she relaxed down onto

his chest. The swing kept swaying with a soft momentum, lulling her into a peaceful state. She hadn't been this calm for quite some time.

Nick's arms wrapped around her, and Silvia kept her eyes shut. She just wanted this moment, with this man.

Whatever problems he shouldered could wait. At this minute, all was right with their world.

Fifteen

"My mother left me a letter."

Nick didn't realize the words were going to slip out until it was too late. But he wasn't sorry. He needed to purge these feelings before they consumed him and turned him into someone he didn't recognize. He hadn't wanted to talk, because saying the truth out loud only made the ugly facts more of a reality.

But Silvia had changed him.

She shifted in his arms. He had no clue how long they'd been lying here completely bare and utterly vulnerable to each other. The sun had set, but he had no desire to move.

"Her attorney gave an envelope to me after her

death," he went on, thankful for the darkness, save for the landscape lights around the pool. "I carried it around for a few days, scared of opening it. I guess I thought if I didn't open it, there was still one more conversation to be had with her. I just didn't want to let that go."

Emotion clogged his throat as Silvia turned. She fisted her hand on his chest and rested her chin on top. He didn't look her in the eye—he couldn't. If he saw pity or sadness from her, he wasn't sure he'd make it through.

"I finally opened it at the cemetery." He cleared his throat, recalling the punch to the gut when he'd first read the words. "She revealed the truth about my biological father."

"You don't seem happy about this news."

Happy? He was utterly disgusted and part of him wished he'd never found out. The other part of him... No, there was no other part. He wished he'd never had to associate himself with Rusty Lockwood, especially not by blood.

"I found out who my biological father is, and he's a total bastard." Nick blew out a sigh, likely from the relief of getting some of this out in the open. "He doesn't know I even exist. Well, I'm sure he knows he has children, but he doesn't know one of them is me."

Silvia flattened her hand against his chest and

pushed up. Now he did look her in the eye, and he wasn't surprised at her wide eyes and open mouth.

"Is it someone here, in Green Valley?" she asked.

Nick nodded. "Rusty Lockwood."

She gasped, which seemed to mirror his gut reaction when he'd discovered the truth, too.

"Now you know why I've been so moody, so out of sorts," he told her. "I guess I'm still in shock myself."

"Are you positive?" she asked. "Did you talk to him?"

Nick glanced back to the starry sky. "I've spoken to him, but not about this. He doesn't know about the letter. I highly doubt he even remembers who my mother was."

There was an anger in him he hadn't realized before. An anger that Rusty could just dismiss Nick's mother like she was nothing and let her fend for herself and the baby they'd made. Men like that literally thought money could solve all of their problems, and Nick believed it had for Rusty for a time. But now, the old man might find himself in too much turmoil and no amount of money could save him.

Nick's arm tightened around Silvia. "I don't know how the hell to be a father. I mean, is it better to have no dad or a terrible dad? I don't even know the answer to that. But I do know I'm going to try to be the best father I can be, because walking away is an immediate failure our child doesn't deserve."

"Oh, Nick."

The sadness in her voice broke him. Tears pricked his eyes, but he blinked them away. Weakness had no place here. Of all the times in his life, this was when he needed to be the strongest—for himself and for his baby. Hell, for Silvia, too. She needed someone stable in her life.

"I don't want pity," he told her, meaning every word. "I'll be there for this baby, but where Rusty is concerned, I battle back and forth on revealing the truth or just keeping it as the ace up my sleeve."

"Are you sure he's really your father?" she asked.

"My mother wouldn't lie about something like that. If she wasn't sure, she never would've told me. And I know that's why she waited until she was gone to let me know. She knew the news would be devastating."

"I don't doubt your ability or your determination to be a great dad. I have no idea what I'm doing in the motherhood department, either. I didn't have the best examples." Silvia sighed. "But with your own father… I don't even know what to say."

"There's nothing to say. I just had to tell someone, and considering I've been a jerk at times, I wanted you to know my mood has nothing to do with you and everything to do with the fact that my life blew up in my face."

Her fingertips skimmed over his bare chest. Her soft, soothing touch affected him in a way he never could have imagined. Maybe hurt recognized hurt. Silvia was the strongest person he knew. She'd been through so much as a child that she was able to listen without judgment. Right now, he didn't necessarily need advice; he needed a sounding board.

"There's more," he told her, sliding his hand over hers on his chest. "My mom mentioned siblings. Brothers."

"What?" She gasped again.

Nick sat up, sending the swing swaying, as he kept her hand clasped against his chest. "I have no idea who they are. She said she sent letters to them as well. At this point, I can wait on brothers to come to my door, or I can confront Rusty and see if he knows anything."

Silvia scooted closer and rested her forehead against his. "I saw you with the letter that day at the cemetery. I wondered what was happening, but I was so consumed with my own problems that I assumed you were just grieving when I saw the pain on your face."

Nick swallowed back his emotions and refused to lose control. "There was so much to take in all at once," he admitted.

"And then I told you I was pregnant."

Yeah, that had been the trifecta of life-altering news. Losing one parent, finding another and learning he was going to be one. Honestly, he was pretty damn proud of himself for holding it all together.

"So what now?" she asked. "Do you want to tell Rusty the truth? Do you want to hire someone to find your brothers?"

Nick eased back and reached up to tuck her hair behind her ear. Trailing his fingertips along her jawline, he watched as she studied him. What he thought earlier had been pity was so much more, so much deeper.

Silvia stared back at him with compassion, determination, as if she was ready to slay those dragons for him. There was nothing sexier or more appealing than a strong woman who wanted to protect her man.

Wait. Her man?

No, that's not what was going on here. He didn't know if he could be a proper father, let alone be in a real relationship with Silvia. He had no experience with either role, and the fear of failing was a serious struggle. She'd had enough people fail her in her life—he didn't want to be added to the long list.

"There's so much I want, I'm not sure where to start with Rusty," he admitted. "But with you, hell, I'm not sure what to do there, either. Do we date? Do we coparent? I'm lost here, Silvia. I know I want you, that much is obvious, but what can I offer you beyond that?"

Silvia's eyes softened. "Nick—"

He framed her face with his hands, stroking his thumb across her bottom lip. Exposing any vulnerability was far removed from his comfort zone, but he also couldn't keep certain feelings to himself.

"I can't be in a public relationship with you," she stated before he could go on. "My career is too important right now. I was just told today there may be a promotion on the line, and that's what I've been working for. If my boss knows that I slept with a client, that I'm carrying a client's baby, I can kiss that promotion goodbye. I bounced around so much from one foster home to the next when I was growing up, not only do I need this career and stability for myself, I need to provide for our baby. I can't be dependent on anyone else."

Anger filled him. On one hand, he understood her drive to want to be at the top of her game and find the success she'd worked so hard for. But the other part of him—the alpha side—wanted to tell her that he would provide everything she or the baby could ever want or need.

"You are human, Silvia," he told her. "I could see if there was a professional issue with our project, but there isn't. I wouldn't cancel contracts with your firm, if that's what they'd be worried about."

Silvia shook her head and scooted off the other side of the swing. Her sudden movements had Nick swaying and confused.

"You don't get it because you're a guy," she insisted. "If a man messed around with a female client, it would seem fun and flirty, but because I'm a woman, and new to the firm, new to town, and I got involved with my very first—and right now only—client, do you know what that will look like to them?"

Once again, anger bubbled up within him, and he swung his legs around to stand.

"Don't say it," he ordered. "Don't think of yourself like that, because I sure as hell don't and anyone who does can go to hell. That firm is damn lucky to have you, and if they don't see it, then they don't deserve you."

Silvia jerked like she was completely shocked at his outburst, at his support of her talents.

"I'm not ready to tell them about the baby," she finally admitted. "Just be patient."

He understood her fears, but he also wanted her to understand that he wouldn't just leave her to fend for herself. Did she worry about abandonment? Because of her upbringing, was she concerned that he'd leave her and the baby?

They were both a mix of strengths and vulnerabilities, and Nick worried the clash might leave them both in a bigger mess than when they'd started.

"Go talk to Rusty," she told him, her tone pleading. "You're going to wrestle these demons until you do. You're not going to get some loving father/son reunion, but at least you'll have the truth out in the open and he can decide what to do from there."

Nick knew at some point he'd have to tell Rusty the truth, as leverage or as closure.

"I don't want to talk about Rusty any more," Nick stated as he circled the swing. "I want to take what I can for now and not worry about anything else... just for a little while."

Silvia's shoulders dropped, the tension visibly leaving her body. She took one step, then another, until she was in his arms.

Nick smoothed her hair down her back, then framed her face and grazed his lips across hers.

"Stay," he murmured. "For as long as you can. Stay."

He found he was always telling her that, and he wondered if this temporary arrangement would slide into permanent.

Nick leaned back in his office chair and stared at the double doors. He'd ordered Rusty to a meeting here, on Nick's turf. Nick knew the old man wouldn't turn down the request. Rusty was too on edge, too worried that Nick might actually have something to make public.

Their volley back and forth was about to come to an end.

"Mr. Lockwood is here to see you."

His assistant's low tone came over the desk speaker, and Nick remained in his seat. He wanted to appear as relaxed as possible, though he felt anything but.

A week had passed since he and Silvia had opened up to each other. She'd been spending her nights with him and going to work the next day. They'd fallen into a regular pattern that seemed natural, perfect.

The double doors opened, and Nick's assistant glanced at him before silently gesturing for Rusty to enter.

"Thank you, Natalie," Nick said. "Why don't you go ahead and take the rest of the day off?"

She smiled and nodded. "Thanks, Nick."

Once she closed the doors, Nick and Rusty were alone. Nick watched as his father glanced around the room, his gaze ultimately landing on Nick.

"You always dismiss employees early on a weekday?"

Nick shrugged and leaned back in his chair. "Happy employees stay loyal, and loyalty keeps the business running smoothly. You run your business the way you want and let me worry about mine," Nick added.

Slowly, he eased from his desk chair and came to his feet. "Care for a drink? I can offer Blanton's, Eagle Rare or Pappy."

"I'm not here for bourbon," Rusty scoffed. "Tell me what you want and let's get this over with."

Nick crossed to his minibar and pulled out a tumbler embossed with his company's logo. He popped the top off a bottle of Hawkins gin and added some tonic and lime. He took his time, purposely irritating his guest.

"Have a seat," Nick said as he crossed back to his desk.

Rusty remained standing near the doorway, but Nick stood by his chair. He held on to the back while gripping his drink in the other hand.

"You ever marry, Rusty?"

Obviously surprised by the opening question, the old man blinked. "Married? No, I didn't. What the hell does that have to do with anything?"

Nick shrugged and took a sip. "Just curious. I believe you knew my mother."

Nick's heart quickened; his palms grew damp. He hated that his mother had had any involvement with this arrogant bastard, but what was done was done.

"Lori Campbell," Nick added after a beat.

Rusty's brows drew in, then he shook his head. "Name doesn't ring a bell. Was she an employee?"

Nick swallowed. "She worked at a hotel you used to own years ago."

He waited for some realization to dawn or any spark of recognition.

Nick gritted his teeth and pulled in a deep breath. "Are you aware of any children you fathered?"

"Children?" Rusty scoffed. "What the hell are you hinting at?"

"I'm your son."

Nick hadn't meant to blurt it out, but he couldn't contain the truth anymore. He set his glass on his desk and stared back at the wide-eyed man.

"Lori Campbell was my mother," Nick stated. "She worked for you, and you got her pregnant."

Rusty's face turned red, his nostrils flaring. "If you think you can blackmail me because of my wealth—"

"Your wealth?" Nick mocked. "I don't give a damn about that. I could buy you out ten times. I care about the fact that you ignored a woman who was having your child. You paid her money to go away, but it wasn't nearly enough and now your past is coming back to haunt you."

Rusty hadn't paid Nick's mother nearly enough. She'd still worked two jobs to make ends meet and looking back on how hard she struggled only pissed Nick off even more.

Rusty took a step forward until he flattened his palms on the desk. "I don't have a son," he ground out. "Any woman I dealt with was compensated. So whatever you're wanting from me now, forget it."

Compensated? Nick nearly felt sick at the thought of this heartless prick paying women to exclude him from the lives of his own children. Nick couldn't imagine how he'd feel about not seeing or knowing his child. How crass would someone have to be to just toss some money and move on?

And that was the obvious difference between

Rusty and him. Maybe they did share the same blood, but Nick wasn't a cold-hearted bastard.

"My mother left me a letter before she passed," Nick stated. "I'm aware that I have half siblings. Do you have any idea who or where they are?"

Rusty pushed off the desk and crossed his arms. "Like I said, I paid enough not to be included in what those women did. I had a business to run and no time for kids running around."

Nick circled his desk until he came to stand directly in front of his nemesis. "I was better off without you in my life. My mother more than filled the void of not having a father, especially a deadbeat dad like you. I wonder what your cronies would think of you paying off women you impregnated. Doesn't sound so noble and loving, like the man you want people to believe you are."

Rusty opened his mouth, but Nick went on, taking another step until he loomed over the pudgy man.

"Couple that with your newly uncovered issue regarding Milestones, and I'd say you have a hell of a scandal on your hands."

If he thought Rusty's face was red before, it was nothing compared to now. He also had a flash of fear in his dark eyes.

"So, do you want to talk about those liquor licenses or are you going to continue to play this game?"

Rusty took a step back. "That's your proof? A letter from a dead woman?"

Nick fisted his hands at his sides and forced himself not to punch the man in the face. "My mother had no reason to lie. In fact, I'm sure she wished anyone else was my father. Why do you think she kept the secret until she was gone? She never wanted to admit she had anything to do with you."

"So you want to blackmail me? Is that it?" Rusty sneered. "Go right ahead. Smaller people have tried to take me down. It comes with being so successful."

Nick snorted. "Bullshit. You're successful because you started out doing something illegal. You've always been crooked—you just hide behind a corporation now. But I'll expose every one of your skeletons if it's the last thing I do. And you can bank on the fact that I'll track down your other children. Your days of running everything in this region are over."

Rusty's lips thinned. "You'll hear from my lawyer."

Nick smiled. "Oh, I'm looking forward to it."

Rusty stormed out, and Nick stared at the open door for a moment before going back to his forgotten drink. He tossed it back and welcomed the refreshing taste of gin with lime.

If Rusty wanted to fight, Nick was more than ready. Nick refused to be a man like Russ—a worthless father, a jerk to the women in his life.

But the fact remained: Rusty was his father, and

Nick had a legitimate fear of that man's blood running through him. Maybe that's why he wasn't ready to commit to Silvia. He didn't even have commitment in his DNA.

Sixteen

Nick slid his hand into Silvia's as they stepped from the doctor's office. She'd had an ultrasound two weeks ago and then her regular visit today. So far, the baby seemed healthy and strong. Nick was still dying to know the gender, but he could wait if that's what Silvia really wanted.

He escorted her toward her car. They'd driven separately, but planned on meeting at the resort site. Still, they couldn't show up together, because she hadn't told her employer they were seeing each other. She'd all but moved her stuff into his place, but she wouldn't just say they were seeing each other.

Not only that, her boss still didn't know she was

expecting a baby. Nick didn't know how much longer he could remain quiet.

Silvia pulled out her keys and released his hand. "Are you heading straight to the site?" she asked, turning to face him.

Nick rested an arm on top of her car. "I'm going to stop and grab something to eat, and then I'll be there. Want me to pick up something for you?"

"I'm good," she told him. "I'm swinging by the office first, and I have some things in my fridge. So, I'll see you there in about an hour?"

Nick pulled in a deep breath and tucked a crimson strand of hair behind her ear. "Maybe you should tell your boss about the baby."

Silvia's eyes widened. "Nick, I will, I just—"

"Need time. You've said that for weeks." He stepped into her and traced a finger down her jawline. "But they're going to find out about the pregnancy and the secret is just added stress that's not good for you or the child. Not to mention you're practically living with me."

"I have my own house," she argued.

"Where you rarely stay," he reminded her. "I don't want them to find out from someone else. That would be much worse than if you just be honest."

"I'll tell them," she promised. "Soon."

"Today?"

She leaned up and slid her lips across his. "Soon," she repeated.

With a pat on his chest, she eased him back so she could open her car door. He watched as she got in and drove from the lot. She was still keeping barriers between them, still worrying about letting him fully in.

He would never be part of her life if he kept his own barriers in place, either. Damn it, he wanted more. Even though something inside him doubted that happiness and long-term commitment were even a possibility.

No, he didn't deserve her, but that didn't mean he didn't want her. Once he'd dealt with all of this mess with his father, his next step would be thinking about moving forward with Silvia.

Rusty had the nerve to block every call and visit, so that wasn't going according to plan. No problem. Nick had a meeting scheduled with the entire city council on Monday morning. The meeting was supposed to be private and secretive, meaning no Rusty, but that didn't mean the shady mogul wouldn't find out.

It was time for action…action in all aspects of his life.

Nick adjusted his glasses and crossed the parking garage toward his SUV. He was ready to take control and claim everything he wanted.

"Are congratulations in order?"

Silvia froze in the midst of grabbing a yogurt from her office refrigerator. Glancing toward the door, she spotted Kevin with a wide smile on his face, holding up his phone, wiggling it like it held some great secret.

Dread curled in her belly as she faced him. Her eyes locked onto the image on the screen, and every fear came crashing down on her.

No. This couldn't be happening.

She'd just left the doctor twenty minutes ago. How could a tabloid already have this photo online?

Silvia stepped closer. Above the image of her and Nick in an intimate embrace beside her car, the headline read, From Mogul to Daddy?

Her eyes scanned the rest of the wording and caught phrases like "mystery lady" and "is Nick Campbell ready to be a dad?" as well as her name and her employer's name. That had been fast detective work from the journalist.

What could she do now? There was no backpedaling and she had no valid excuse as to why she'd kept the secret.

"I had no idea," Kevin continued, oblivious to the turmoil spiraling through her. "And Nick Campbell? Girl, you wasted no time. Does Clark know you guys are…well, you know?"

Silvia's mind whirled. She hadn't even seen anyone lurking, but she also hadn't been looking for anyone, either.

Nobody even knew there was a secret to be kept other than her and Nick. He'd lingered by her car for longer than usual. Had he been giving the photographer time to get the perfect shot?

She didn't think he'd do this, but who else would have anything to gain from exposing their relationship?

Maybe Nick wasn't the man she'd hoped he could be. She'd been disappointed before by those she'd cared about.

"Excuse me," Silvia said, pushing past Kevin.

She had to get to Clark's office now. If he saw that image or if another employee got to him first, Silvia would have a difficult time explaining why she'd not come forward sooner. She'd been working with Nick for nearly six months, but she didn't know if Clark would believe that the affair started less than two months ago.

Her heart beat quickened with each step she took toward her boss's office. She should've been up front with Clark from the beginning. But she'd been so afraid of either losing her job or losing her heart. Because she'd known that the moment she admitted she was pregnant, the discussion would've snowballed and revealed the identity of the baby's father.

Silvia had so many reasons why she hadn't wanted to tell people, but right at this minute, they all seemed irrelevant. How could she provide financial security and stability for her child if she was out of a job?

She pulled in a deep breath as she reached Clark's double doors. When she tapped on them, they eased open, and there was Clark's assistant beside his desk with his phone. The way both men glanced up at her, she knew.

"Well, Silvia, come on in," Clark greeted. "I was just reading some fascinating news about you. And I assume congratulations are in order."

"Thank you, sir."

His assistant pocketed his cell and excused himself, leaving Silvia and Clark alone. She'd never been this nervous or anxious in her life.

"I had planned to tell you about my condition," she started the moment they had privacy. "Since I'm new here and my pregnancy was unplanned, I was trying to find the right time."

"Understandable," Clark agreed as he eased back in his seat. "And I really did mean congratulations on your pregnancy. I have five children of my own and three grandchildren. They're a blessing. I have no qualms about the pregnancy whatsoever. I do, however, have issues with you getting involved with a client while you're working on his project. One of the firm's most prestigious projects, actually."

Silvia clasped her hands in front of her and remained still. Her heart beat so hard, her stomach curled with tension and knots. But she wasn't going to show fear or worry, because she needed to remain strong, not just for her future, but for her boss to see she was an asset to this company.

"We don't condone this type of behavior," Clark

went on. "It's not my business what you do in your spare time, but it is my business when it involves our biggest client. I can't exactly let this pass."

Silvia nodded. "I understand your concern, sir, but I assure you that my involvement with Mr. Campbell will not reflect on this company and will not hinder the project."

"This is already going to affect the company because of the media coverage," he countered. "You know how fast and far these stories travel."

"I also know that the next story will come along and mine will be forgotten," she informed him. "You just commended me on my performance and on how well I'm doing. Let me continue to do well for this company and prove what an asset I am to you."

He stared at her, his gaze unwavering, and she wanted nothing more than to run from the room and find out who was responsible for making that photo public. But she had to fight this battle with Clark first, before she could move on.

"Why don't you take a week off—paid, of course," he quickly added. "Let's see what happens and if there's backlash. This firm has a remarkable reputation, and I cannot allow my newest employee to tarnish what I've worked so hard to attain."

A week off? She didn't like the sound of that. He was making her feel like she'd done something wrong when all she'd done was fall into the arms of a man she'd been unable to resist. There was no policy here against fraternizing with clients. She'd only wanted to be extra cautious by keeping it secret. Was being human with basic needs wrong? Had she not gotten pregnant, her boss never would've known about her sex life, but now it was suddenly all over social media and fodder for office gossip.

"You should know I have an impeccable reputation as well," she added, more than ready to defend herself. "I'll be back in one week, and I will continue to do my job with as much excellence as always. The client I'm working with and all of my future clients will not care about my private life and you, sir, shouldn't, either."

She'd never normally talk disrespectfully to the one who signed her paycheck, but she also needed to stand her ground. She wasn't sorry for her actions. She hadn't left a black mark on the company, and she'd bet that if she started digging, she'd find at least one employee who'd had a fling with a client.

"I'll see you next week," she told him as she turned on her heel and walked calmly out the door, shoulders back and head high.

Her walk down the hall was quick. Whispers filtered from offices, but she didn't glance around. She didn't care who was talking about her, because she had bigger problems to worry about than what gossipmongers were saying. They had no effect on her life. Finding out who had shattered her small bubble of trust took precedence right now.

She had a week, right? Well, Silvia figured she'd find the culprit in the next few minutes…as soon as she met him at the site.

If he wasn't the man she'd thought he was, what would she do? She wasn't sure how she could raise a child with someone she couldn't trust. She knew he was all alpha, wanting to provide for her and take care of her.

Had he let this secret out as a way to make sure she needed to lean on him even more?

Silvia was about to find out.

Seventeen

Nick walked through the third floor, examining all the new framework for the suites. He glanced at his phone again and wondered what was keeping Silvia. It wasn't like her to be late, but maybe something had held her up at work.

He bypassed the second floor, where the crew was working for the day, and went down to the main lobby. Still no sign of her, so he headed toward the back of the building and stepped out onto the expansive wraparound deck with breathtaking views. This was where they would host parties and private receptions and even weddings. His mother had created a very detailed packaging plan for guests. He couldn't wait to see the end result come to fruition.

Out of all the businesses he'd worked on, this was by far his favorite. Unlike those others, which he'd flipped and sold, this one he would keep forever. Perhaps his child would want to take over this resort one day. Maybe this could be the start of a legacy. Nothing would've made his mother happier than to know her grandchild would one day take the reins.

A thrill of hope about a future with Silvia burst through him. What would she say if he asked her to create that family, that dynasty? With her architectural skills and his business sense, they could create a hell of a company. Of course, they could stay based out of Green Valley, but traveling with their child and exploring the world and flipping old buildings into something grand would be amazing.

And maybe that's the dream he'd been waiting for. Maybe that was the life that had been calling to him. He'd just had to find the right woman to share it with.

Nick knew his mother would've loved having a grandchild, and she likely would have been gooey and all smiles over how Nick and Silvia had found each other in the most difficult of circumstances. Now he just had to convince Silvia that they were right for each other, that her past didn't have to dictate her future.

Nick stared out over the mountains and instantly envisioned a wedding here. His wedding to his beautiful bride, glowing with pregnancy.

He smiled, unable to prevent happiness from

bursting out. He loved Silvia. Maybe he'd been falling in love from the moment he'd met her, but now he knew he didn't want to be without her.

Raising their child in the kind of home they'd both missed out on would be their ultimate testimony to love and commitment.

And knowing he was building an even bigger legacy than he'd ever dreamed filled him with a burst of hope. He truly wished his mother could be here to see everything.

"Tell me you didn't leak the story."

Nick jerked around. Silvia stood in the open doorway, her wide eyes locked on his.

"What?" he asked.

"The story splashed all over social media." She pulled her phone from her pocket and held the screen out to him. "Did you do this?"

Confused, Nick closed the distance between them and took her phone. He stared at the photo of them, obviously taken just a while ago outside the doctor's office when Nick had been easing her hair behind her ears. There was another shot of when he'd kissed her.

The headlines, the comments, the hashtags—all were claiming the business mogul was becoming a father, and Silvia's name was mentioned, as well as the name of her firm.

His eyes darted back to hers and there was no mistaking she was serious about her accusations.

"I told you I would tell them," she insisted. "I told you to give me time. Why would you do this?"

"Wait. You truly think I did this?"

He waited for her to deny it, but the way she stared at him with so much hurt and anger, he could see she truly had convinced herself that he'd had a hand in outing them.

Did she immediately think the worst of him because of his confession about his biological father? Rusty was a total bastard, but Nick worked damn hard not to be like that. He'd always tried to be straightforward and honest, even more so now that he knew the genes he fought against.

"Who else even knew we had a secret?" she asked, her arms out wide. "I certainly didn't have someone ready to take our picture outside my OB's office. I assume you wanted a valid reason for me to rely on you, a reason for me to let you do everything for me like you wanted to do from the start. You thought a few pics and a clever headline would get the truth out there and speed that process along."

Nick didn't know what feeling lay so heavy on his heart, but it certainly wasn't the happiness and hope that had been there only moments ago.

"And you really believe I did this?" he asked again, giving her another chance to say something else.

"Did you?" she asked.

Nick pulled in a slow breath and glanced around

at the mountains. That image he'd had of the two of them pledging their lives to each other had vanished.

He focused his attention back onto her. A fresh new slice of pain hit him hard. Maybe he was fighting a battle inside himself over what it meant to find out he was Rusty Lockwood's son, but that struggle didn't mean he would purposely, maliciously hurt someone he loved.

"The fact that you're even asking me really crumbles every ounce of trust I've built with you."

Her eyes widened, then closed. She blew out a sigh and shook her head.

"My first thought was that you planted someone there so it would pop up on social media and hopefully get back to my boss—which it did, by the way."

Nick eased his hurt aside for a moment, concerned with her well-being. "What did he say?"

"I was given a week's paid leave until they see if there's going to be a scandal or a smear on the firm's reputation."

Nick's fury volleyed between Silvia's mistrust of him and her dumb-ass boss not believing in her. How dare that man say something to her about the relationship she had outside of work hours? Yes, Clark had a reputation to uphold, but he also had to be considerate to his employees and treat them all equally.

"If you tell me you didn't do this," she said, "then I'll believe you."

Nick shoved his hands in his pockets and stared

back at her. "I don't have to say anything," he told her, the hurt growing deeper and deeper. "You either know my character or you don't. And the fact that my betrayal was your first suspicion says nothing about me, but a lot about you and your fears about us."

She jerked as if he'd smacked her.

"I didn't leak anything," he went on, forcing himself to close down the anguish he was feeling and just be honest. "I'm as blindsided as you are."

Silvia's bright blue eyes filled. "You can't blame me for wondering if you had something to do with those photos. The timing was too perfect."

"Maybe it was perfect," he agreed, a gnawing ache settling deep. That fear that maybe he wouldn't ever be good enough for long-term, that he and Silvia weren't meant for each other, consumed him. "But if you'd taken just a few seconds to think before jumping to a damning conclusion, we wouldn't be in this spot now."

"And what's that spot?" she whispered, one tear spilling down her cheek.

Unable to stop himself, Nick reached out and swiped away the moisture. He hadn't known it possible to physically hurt so badly from being heartbroken. The loss of his mother, the discovery of his father, now this. It was all too much.

"Back at the beginning, where we don't fully trust each other," he answered, dropping his hand. "Go take that week of vacation, but I can't be part of it. I can't make you happy. I'll be around if you need to tell me anything about the baby, but other than that, I can't be with you, Sil. It's too painful to love you and know you don't believe I'm the man you deserve."

He moved around her and walked through the lobby and out the front door. He bounded down the steps and straight to his truck. His vision blurred as tears pricked his eyes, and he blinked them away.

Over the past few weeks, there had been so many emotions that had completely taken over. He had no idea when he'd ever feel completely whole again or how he'd get his life back on the track he needed it to be.

All he knew was he'd never hurt like this. Between his mother and now Silvia, there was only so much pain he could handle.

Nick pulled away from the site and gripped the wheel as he tried to keep his emotions in check. How could she believe he'd ever do such a thing, especially after she'd told him how important it was for her to keep things secret?

All he could assume was that she truly didn't know him, and having such a vengeful, wicked man as his father didn't help his case. Hadn't Nick believed all along that he wasn't good enough for her? He'd wanted to prove himself—he'd even gotten his damn heart involved when he'd known good and well that was a mistake.

Nick found himself driving toward Silvia's firm

before he realized what he was doing, but since she'd had her say with them, Nick figured he wanted his, too. He was their client, after all, and his working relationship with Silvia was the reason for her paid time off.

As Nick pulled into a parking spot, his cell chimed. He killed the engine and picked up his phone. Rusty's name lit up the screen, and Nick swiped open the message.

Immediately the photo that had surfaced on social media filled the screen, and Rusty's message read, Like father like son.

Rage bubbled within Nick, and he shot off a reply.

I take responsibility...like mother like son.

He put his cell on silent and stepped from his truck. He didn't need that reminder that there could be any of Rusty's negative traits inside Nick. He'd been raised by the strongest, most amazing woman ever. She had done all the parenting, so there should be no trace of Rusty inside of Nick.

Ignoring his niggle of worry about somehow ending up like his father, Nick went straight in the main doors of the office and requested to see Clark immediately. The receptionist—Kevin, if Nick recalled—fumbled with the phone and made a quick call. Apparently, Nick's face gave him away. It must have revealed that he wasn't going to wait and he wasn't here for small talk.

"You can go on up," Kevin stated as he hung up the phone.

Nick nodded his thanks and moved to the elevators. Moments later, he marched through the fourth floor of the firm and straight to Clark's office, where the doors were open.

"Nick," Clark greeted as he came to his feet. "Great to see you. Come on in."

Nick stepped in and shook the man's hand. "I'm sure you know why I'm here."

"I can guess," Clark replied, then gestured toward the bar along the wall. "Can I offer you a drink?"

"I won't be long," Nick stated. "I just want to make it clear that if Silvia is taken off this project or if she is removed from her position here, I promise, I will take my business on this project and all future projects elsewhere."

Clark's smile vanished. "I gave Silvia a week off with paid leave."

"I'm aware of that," Nick stated, refusing to back down on this topic. "I'm also aware that's your way of figuring out what to do with her. It's your business, of course, and you can do what you want, but I'm just making my position clear. So you know where *my* business stands on the matter. I'm positive you could find another employee who had an outside relationship with a client. Your firm is too large—you've done too many projects. Silvia's not your first."

Clark's jaw clenched. "I'll take your words under advisement. Thanks for stopping in."

Nick knew that was his cue to go, which was fine. He'd come for what he wanted, and he'd made his case clear. He also knew Silvia wouldn't like that he had come to her defense here, but he didn't give a damn. His name was associated with this story as well as hers, and even though he was angry with her, she still deserved to have someone standing in her corner. She'd never had that, and damn it, he loved her.

No matter what went down between them or where they landed, he couldn't just turn off his emotions.

Besides that, she'd worked too hard for her career, and she deserved to do the job she excelled at.

As Nick marched back to his car, the message from Rusty slid to the front of his mind, and Nick knew in that instant who had leaked the story. That's something Rusty would do—underhanded, scheming, having Nick followed to look for dirt.

Nick didn't care, though. The truth would have come out eventually, and if Rusty thought this would make Nick back down, Rusty was an even bigger fool than Nick had thought.

He headed back to his house. With his heart so heavy, he'd rather work from home than deal with any employees or questions…especially today. No doubt if any of his staff had popped onto social media, they would've seen the pictures.

Right now, all he could do was focus on the resort, like his mother wanted. Silvia and that stab of betrayal would have to take a back seat in his mind—and in his heart.

Eighteen

Silvia walked into the spare bedroom and flicked on the light. She'd tried to go to bed around midnight, but thoughts kept swirling around in her mind. Between her boss, the baby and Nick, her entire world had been flipped every which way. She honestly didn't know what to do next.

After two hours of staring into the darkness, she decided to come into the room she'd envisioned as the nursery. Right now, she utilized this space as a library. She'd put up an entire wall of shelves. The bay window made a perfect lounge area to curl up and read…not that she'd had much time to do that lately.

She padded barefoot across the plush pale pink rug and took a seat on the window cushion. Silvia grabbed a fluffy white throw pillow and hugged it to her chest as she stared out at the starry sky and the full moon over the mountains.

Sleep wasn't going to come any time soon for her. Whether her eyes were open or shut, all she saw was that pain in Nick's eyes. She hadn't flat out accused him, but her question had made it seem that way. He'd told her she should've known his character enough to trust that he wouldn't betray her. And she did. Damn it, she did. Nick was the nicest, most considerate, most protective person she'd ever met in her life. How could she think—even for a moment, even when all evidence seemed to point his way—that he would purposely hurt her?

Everything he'd said had been accurate. She was afraid of happiness. She'd never fully had that in her life before now, and she wasn't sure how to react.

All of which were lame excuses for being so hurtful to the one man she loved.

And she did love him.

Silvia hadn't heard from or seen Nick in three days. She was absolutely miserable. Her bed was lonely; her days were lonely. She desperately missed him.

She also hadn't heard a word from Clark, which really irked her. The longer she thought about her position at his firm and his response to her pregnancy, the more she re-evaluated what she wanted. She really wanted to work for a prestigious firm, but more so, she wanted to be proud of herself at the end of the day. Her work was damn good, and she wasn't vain in thinking that. Nick and his mother wouldn't have hired her if they hadn't liked her portfolio.

Silvia had decisions to make. She could continue to be miserable without Nick and go back to work in four days for a man who might or might not still be thinking she was the black sheep of the office. Or she could take control of that happiness she'd found, apologize to Nick and see what this next chapter of life would bring her way.

Silvia stared around the room and wondered what Nick would want to do…if he forgave her. Would he want to live here or in the home he'd built? Would he want to work with her on more projects after this resort?

There was no guarantee he'd trust her again. He'd said they were back at square one. But Silvia was going to push aside her fear of heartache and let herself love him.

Nick had been hurt, too, and he had freely opened himself to her. Then what had she done? She'd taken his vulnerable heart and crushed it. Knowing she'd hurt him only made her insomnia that much worse. She couldn't stand knowing he was likely still in pain when he'd never done anything but lift her up and encourage her, all while dealing with the death of his mother.

Silvia rested her cheek on the throw pillow and figured she'd have to get some sleep so she could tackle her new attitude and new life goals come morning.

She couldn't help but feel a slight burst of hope. Clark and Nick wouldn't have a clue who this new Silvia was… She just prayed she was making the right decision where all parties and her future were concerned.

Nick adjusted his tie and stared at his reflection. Yesterday morning he'd received a text from Silvia requesting that he meet her at the airport wearing black-tie attire. She'd told him she had some news. She'd added that she knew she didn't deserve for him to show up, but she was just asking for a few minutes.

He had no clue what she planned to tell him or why he had to be dressed up to hear it, but there was no way he would miss this meeting. He'd been damn lonely without her. When he'd had dinner last night, Nick had eaten three pieces of bread and realized he should have one more, to make it even.

It was memories of those silly little quirks that filled his days. That wide smile of hers that would make her eyes glisten. He missed her in his bed, in his home, hanging by the fire outside late into the night. He missed everything about her.

Receiving her text had been the biggest relief.

He wanted the chance to apologize for the way he'd reacted. Instead of talking things through, he'd ended it and walked away. That's not the man he wanted to be, and that's sure as hell not the man she deserved. He was ready to prove he could be the man for her.

Nick had given her space, given her time to think. He'd hoped she would come around, but he didn't want to push. Silvia needed to come to every conclusion on her own, and Nick knew she was strong enough to do just that.

Her only flaw? Fear.

Well, he'd been scared, too. Scared she wouldn't come back, scared she'd push him away for good, scared she would throw away all they could've been.

So he hoped this text and meet up was about their future.

Nick stopped fidgeting with his tie and grabbed his keys and phone. Twenty minutes later he pulled into the lot that housed his plane.

He gasped as he took in the scene before him. His Cessna had been pulled out onto the runway. A mini runway of candles ran from the parking lot to the plane, where Silvia stood. His breath caught again at the sight of her in a strapless white dress with her red hair down and curled around her shoulders.

Nick parked and stepped from his SUV then made his way down the path of flickering candles toward Silvia.

"Did you pull my plane out?" he asked when he reached her.

"Don't be mad," she told him, wrinkling her nose out of nerves. "I called the manager of the airport and incorporated his help."

Mad? He wasn't mad. Intrigued? Definitely.

"And what do you have planned that you need my plane?" he asked, sliding his hands into his pockets to keep from reaching for her.

"You said I should know your character. So I'm counting on the fact that you said you love me. I'm counting on you giving me another chance even though I don't deserve it. I'm counting on you taking me on this plane and going to a destination I chose and filed in your flight plan."

Shocked and more than impressed, Nick took another step toward her. Now he did reach out, smoothing her hair from her shoulders. She was so damn breathtaking, he could hardly stand it. Being away from her for any amount of time had been pure hell.

"I know your character," she went on. "I know you're the best thing that's ever happened to me. I know you're going to be the best father to our baby, because you push when you should and you give me space when I'm being a jerk."

"It wasn't me that leaked the pregnancy," he told her. "It was Rusty. I'm dealing with him in my own way, on my own time, but he had a photographer following me trying to dig up dirt on me for blackmail."

"I'm sorry he's your father," Silvia murmured. "Sorry he's causing you more hurt."

Yeah, he was sorry, too, but that wasn't important now. Rusty had no place here, in this moment, and Nick would definitely deal with him later.

He framed her face and smoothed the pad of his thumb over her bottom lip.

"I also know you went and talked to Clark," she added with a quirk of her brow. "You know I can take care of myself, but that was sweet in a protective sort of way."

"Clark and his firm don't deserve you," he told her.

Silvia smiled. "No, they don't. Which is why I plan on turning in my resignation. Now, don't worry, I'm working on a few plans. I don't intend to be unemployed and living off your wealth."

Nick couldn't stop his grin. "Is that right?"

"I paid for this little trip, though, so that's not on you," she stated. "But I do need you to fly this plane, because I'm not quite that good."

"And where are we going?" He closed the minuscule distance between them, making their bodies line up perfectly. "Because I'm fine with going back to my house and showing you a little more about my character."

Silvia curled her hands around his neck. "We're taking a trip first, because we need to talk, and we need to get away."

Hope overcame him for the first time since they'd fought. "I agree. I'm sorry for how I treated you the other day. That's not who I want to be for you."

Her fingertips threaded through his hair. "I know that's not the real you, just like me assuming the worst in you isn't the real me."

Nick feathered his lips across hers, unable to stop himself from seeking more of her touch, her affection.

"I can't stay angry with you when you were only running because you were afraid," he murmured against her mouth. "You had a terrible childhood, but I'm here to make sure the rest of your life is nothing but happiness and memories you want to keep."

She eased back with a wide smile. "That's going to go really well with my plan."

"And what plan is that?"

"What do you say about a quick flight to the coast, a wedding at sunrise and then…who knows?"

Nick stilled, his heart kicking up at the prospect of being with Silvia forever. "A wedding?"

Silvia stepped back and took his hands in hers. "Will you marry me? Can we be that family neither of us had? Can we grow more and more in love each day with our baby?"

Nick laughed. "I can't believe you're proposing to me."

Her smile faltered. "Does that mean you don't want—"

He scooped her up off her feet and spun her around. "Don't finish that sentence," he commanded with a quick smack on her lips. "I'll marry you anywhere at any time. But a beach wedding sounds perfect. How did you pull all of this off? Were you sure I'd say yes?"

"I pulled some strings," she informed him, her

smile so wide it stole his breath. "And I told you, I know your character. I was certain you'd say yes."

Nick kissed her, claiming the woman he'd always wanted but hadn't known he'd been missing.

"I love you, Silvia."

She rested her head on his chest. "I love you, Nick. I just have one stop on our way to the coast."

"What's that?"

She focused her eyes back on his. "Double Down Donuts has a special order for us in lieu of a wedding cake."

Nick's heart swelled. "You thought of everything."

"I thought it was a way to include your mother in the day. The owner is making her favorite donut into a double stack cake."

"Double," he repeated. "Of course."

"There's only one thing I want one of," she told him.

"What's that?"

She kissed him. "One lifetime with you."

* * * * *

Will Nick meet his half brothers? Find out in the next two books of the Lockwood Lightning trilogy:
Scandalous Reunion
available May 2020
and
Scandalous Engagement
available June 2020

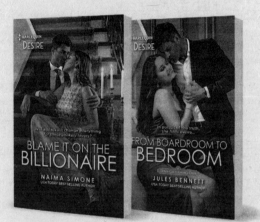

SPECIAL EXCERPT FROM

ⒽHARLEQUIN
DESIRE

Putting family first, CEO Joshua Lowell abandoned his dreams to save his father's empire. When journalist Sophie Armstrong uncovers a shocking secret, he'll do everything in his power to shield his family and his pride from another scandal. But wanting her is a complication he didn't foresee...

Read on for a sneak peek at
Ruthless Pride
by USA TODAY *bestselling author Naima Simone*

"Stalking me, Ms. Armstrong?" he drawled, his fingers gripping his water bottle so tight, the plastic squeaked in protest.

He immediately loosened his hold. Damn, he'd learned long ago to never betray any weakness of emotion. People were like sharks scenting bloody chum in the water when they sensed a chink in his armor. But when in this woman's presence, his emotions seemed to leak through like a sieve. The impenetrable shield barricading him that had been forged in the fires of pain, loss and humiliation came away dented and scratched after an encounter with Sophie. And that presented as much of a threat, a danger to him, as her insatiable need to prove that he was a deadbeat father and puppet to a master thief.

"Stalking you?" she scoffed, bending down to swipe her own bottle of water and a towel off the ground. "Need I remind you, it was you who showed up at my job yesterday, not the other way around. So I guess that makes us even in the showing-up-where-we're-not-wanted department."

"Oh, we're not even close to anything that resembles even, Sophie," he said, using her name for the first time aloud. And damn if it didn't taste good on his tongue. If he didn't sound as if he were stroking the two syllables like they were bare, damp flesh.

"I hate to disappoint you and your dreams of narcissistic grandeur, but I've been a member of this gym for years." She swiped her towel over her throat and upper chest. "I've seen you here, but it's not my fault if you've never noticed me."

"That's bull," he snapped. "I would've noticed you."

The words echoed between them, the meaning in them pulsing like a thick, heavy heartbeat in the sudden silence that cocooned them. Her silver eyes flared wide before they flashed with...what? Surprise? Irritation? Desire. A liquid slide of lust prowled through him like a hungry—so goddamn hungry—beast.

The air simmered around them. How could no one else see it shimmer in waves from the concrete floor like steam from a sidewalk after a summer storm?

She was the first to break the visual connection, and when she ducked her head to pat her arms down, the loss of her eyes reverberated in his chest like a physical snapping of tautly strung wire. He fisted his fingers at his side, refusing to rub the echo of soreness there.

"Do you want me to pull out my membership card to prove that I'm not some kind of stalker?" She tilted her head to the side. "I'm dedicated to my job, but I refuse to cross the line into creepy…or criminal."

He ground his teeth against the apology that shoved at his throat, but after a moment, he jerked his head down in an abrupt nod. "I'm sorry. I shouldn't have jumped to conclusions." And then because he couldn't resist, because it still gnawed at him when he shouldn't have cared what she—a reporter—thought of him or not, he added, "That predilection seems to be in the air."

She narrowed her eyes on him, and a tiny muscle ticked along her delicate but stubborn jaw. Why that sign of temper and forced control fascinated him, he opted not to dwell on. "And what is that supposed to mean?" she asked, the pleasant tone belied by the anger brewing in her eyes like gray storm clouds.

Moments earlier, he'd wondered if fury or desire had heated her gaze.

God help him, because masochistic fool that he'd suddenly become, he craved them both.

He wanted her rage, her passion…wanted both to beat at him, heat his skin, touch him. Make him feel.

Mentally, he scrambled away from that, that need, like it'd reared up and flashed its fangs at him. The other man he'd been—the man who'd lost himself in passion, paint and life captured on film—had drowned in emotion. Willingly. Joyfully. And when it'd been snatched away—when that passion, that life—had been stolen from him by cold, brutal reality, he'd nearly crumbled under the loss, the darkness. Hunger, wanting something so desperately, led only to the pain of eventually losing it.

He'd survived that loss once. Even though it'd been like sawing off his own limbs. He might be an emotional amputee, but dammit, he'd endured. He'd saved his family, their reputation and their business. But he'd managed it by never allowing himself to need again.

And Sophie Armstrong, with her pixie face and warrior spirit, wouldn't undo all that he'd fought and silently screamed to build.

Don't miss what happens next in…
Ruthless Pride *by Naima Simone,*
the first in the Dynasties: Seven Sins series,
where passion may be the only path to redemption.

Available May 2020 wherever
Harlequin Desire books and ebooks are sold.

Harlequin.com

HDEXP0420

Get 4 FREE REWARDS!

We'll send you 2 FREE Books plus 2 FREE Mystery Gifts.

Harlequin Desire® books transport you to the world of the American elite with juicy plot twists, delicious sensuality and intriguing scandal.

FREE Value Over $20